MW00934999

Washington's Doubloon

Frank R. Faunce

For more information about *Washington's Doubloon*, its characters, the book's authors, and other works, visit the author website at

www.frankfaunce.com

This is a work of fiction. Names, characters, places, and incidents either are the product of the author's imagination or are used fictitiously. Any resemblance to actual persons, living or dead, events, or locales is entirely coincidental.

Copyright © 2018 Frank R. Faunce

All rights reserved.

Cover design by Mike McDowell

Interior design by Kerry Faunce

ISBN-13: 978-1723579998
ISBN-10: 1723579998

FOREWORD

In *Washington's Doubloon*, the author has woven together historical facts and legends about the gift of a Brasher Doubloon to President George Washington and the legend of the lost treasure of the Knights Templar to offer a plausible explanation for the question, "How did America pay off all its debts after the Revolutionary War and actually end up with a surplus?"

The historical facts are that there are only seven Brasher Doubloons known to exist today, and Washington's Doubloon is one of them—but which one?

The Brasher Doubloon was the first of a series of gold coins minted by the United States when George Washington became the first president of the new nation. Ephraim Brasher designed the first coin. He was a gold and silversmith and a next-door neighbor of George Washington in New York City when the United States Capitol was first located there.

As the story goes, a secret letter from Brasher was sent to George Washington to be handed down to future presidents describing a valuable gift to the new nation he described as the "New Jerusalem on the Potomac." The letter also mentioned their mutual friends and brother Freré *Maçons* Alexander Hamilton and Major General Arthur Sinclair, the fifteenth president of the Continental Congress and the first governor of the Old Northwest Territory.

It was believed by some ancient historians that the hidden Templar treasure was brought to the New World by Prince Henry Saint Clair in 1398. Eighteen ships containing the silver, gold, and other treasures of the Templars left La Rochelle harbor in France in 1307. Six of the ships simply disappeared and the other twelve made it to Edinburgh, Scotland. The treasure was believed to be buried at Saint Mary Chapel in Scotland.

Prince Henry was charged in 1396 by Queen Margarette with the mission to fulfill Leif Erickson's dream of creating a new kingdom in Vinland. It is thought that the Knights Templar treasure was taken to New Jerusalem in the New World by Prince Henry where Queen Margarette, ruler of Norway, Sweden, and Denmark, intended to create new trade routes with her new colony of New Jerusalem.

Prince Henry's ships carrying soldiers, knights, Cistercian priests, and settlers to her new colony were befriended by the Mi'qmaq Indians in what is now known as Nova Scotia. Queen Margarette's envisioned colony stretched from south of Hudson Bay to Nova Scotia, south to the Mississippi delta, and east to Florida, encompassing the east coast of America and Canada. Rüne stone markers, each with a hooked X, have been found that mark these boundaries of her colony.

When Queen Margarette was assassinated by her enemy, the Hanseatic League, the settlement was abandoned by her son and heir, and the settlers hid the treasure. Legend has it that only the Mi'qmaq chiefs and their successors know one of the important clues to the secret of the vast treasure and its hiding place.

In this novel, the third in a trilogy by the author, the search for the treasure of the Knights Templar intertwines with the enigmatic reference to the "New Jerusalem on the Potomac" and the message sent to George Washington. It makes for a plausible history mystery of the first order.

This is a story of intrigue and a credible solution to a historical puzzle surrounding the newly formed United States. You will be amazed at the cleverness of these adventurers as they use their wits to escape the deadly intent of the Muslim Brotherhood.

Although the books in the trilogy are historical fiction, you will enjoy identifying and following the eleven clues that build on each other in this last book to lead the reader to the hidden Templar treasure that began in the first book of the series, *"Mystery at the Thirteen Sycamores,"* and continued through *"The Seton Secret"* to *"Washington's Doubloon."*

The author and his colleague, Dr. Joe Rudé, have spent years researching and documenting the materials used for this trilogy.

I have known and had the pleasure of working with the author on a variety of projects for many years, the most notable of which were the educational efforts to introduce general dentists to laminate veneers developed and patented by the author.

Often an author reveals his/herself in the interaction of the characters and the settings in their books. In this novel the reader becomes aware that the author is a renaissance man, if you will, who is very knowledgeable in medieval and early American history, the sciences, arts, literature, travel, and adventure.

The kind and thoughtful manner in which the characters interact with each other and the role of women as active participants in solving the mysteries in the trilogy are indicative of his relationships with others.

Fran S. Watkins, Ed.D.
Dame, Hospitaller Order of Saint John of Jerusalem

PREFACE

If you have ever wondered why one coin would be worth $7.6 million and why only seven Brasher Doubloons have ever been found, then this book is for you! Another question that may also be asked about the Brasher Doubloons is why was the first doubloon minted different from all the others? Ephraim Brasher, a lieutenant in the New York Militia and the Revolutionary Continental Army and friend of George Washington was also a goldsmith and a silversmith who made silverware for George Washington when he was president of the United States. He was also the designer of the first gold coin from the United States Mint - the Brasher Doubloon!

The first Brasher Doubloon had Ephraim Brasher's initials on the American shield over the breast of the American eagle on the face side of the coin with the motto of the United States, Unum E Pluribus encircling the eagle. The obverse side had an image of Mount Marcy and a lake with New York State's motto Excelsior followed by Nova Eboraca Columbia encircling it. All the other doubloons have Brasher's initials on the eagle's right wing. Mount Marcy is the highest mountain in New York and the lake is Mirror Lake at Lake Placid. From Lake Placid, one can see Mount Marcy which resembles a pyramid.

Why out of all of the millions of doubloons minted has only seven been discovered? And why did Ephraim Brasher, who lived next door to George Washington on Cherry Street in New York City during the first year of his presidency, send a secret letter to George Washington when he could have just walked next door and talked or given it to him?

Ephraim Brasher was also friends with Alexander Hamilton, the first secretary of the Treasury, and friends with Major General Arthur Saint Clair who was once in the British Army but migrated to America before the Revolutionary War and when it broke out, helped fund the Revolutionary War. He was a president of the Continental Congress for a year and a major general on George Washington's staff and first governor of the Old Northwest Territory after the war. He was married to Phoebe Bayard from a prominent Boston family. He was born in Thurso, Scotland, and descended from Prince Henry Saint Clair, grandfather of William Saint Clair who built Rosslyn Chapel. He was also distantly related to the wife of Christopher Columbus!

The United States had a temporary income tax under the War Powers Act during the emergency of the Civil War, but not until an amendment to the Constitution in 1913 was passed by the states did the first income tax law become legal in 1914 and the Internal Revenue Service was created to enforce it.

After the Revolutionary War, the Louisiana Purchase by Thomas Jefferson and the War of 1812, the United States had encumbered a terrific national debt. Amazingly, by 1835 - 1838, the United States became debt free. How was that possible? It wasn't until the terrible polarizing of people's attitudes toward slavery and states' rights leading to the Civil War in 1860 did the United States begin to amass another period of national debt that today has grown to an accumulated overwhelming $21 trillion. This debt is still climbing despite an income tax and increasing taxes on all fronts.

This is amazing, in view of a Revolutionary War that began as a revolt against a stamp and tea tax by England. The public then as now might say, "Enough is enough - taxation without representation!"

This book is a lost treasure quest that delves into the origins of a dream by a queen who wanted to create a new country named New Jerusalem with the aid of the wealth and spirit of the Knights Templar sequestered within the Hospitaller Order of Saint John of Jerusalem in Scotland, Wales, and Ireland. This dream over the centuries has morphed into what has been called, The Shining City on a Hill - the United States of America!

Frank R. Faunce

ACKNOWLEDGMENTS

The dream that Dr. Joe Rudé and I had many years ago was to tell the story of the Hospitaller Order of Saint John of Jerusalem and the Knights Templar sequestered within that Order as the Fréré Maçons in Ireland, Scotland, and Wales for protection from the Inquisition and seizure of their properties by various monarchs. This history has been expressed in context of a trilogy of fictitious mystery, thriller, and adventure novels.

Joe and I have spent over fifteen years of careful historical research in many libraries, books and documents in many countries including Canada, the United Kingdom, Europe, Middle East, Africa, and the United States to develop the background for these novels that I hope you will enjoy and perhaps learn some history.

I would be remiss if I didn't acknowledge the contributions and encouragement of many of our friends in the various modern Hospitaller Orders of Saint John of Jerusalem and Knights Templar that are descended from those ancient Orders, not to mention classmates and friends whose personas are represented by the characters in these books.

Modern mystery novels that share real history and facts are more exciting than pure fiction. This novel, like the two others in this trilogy, is based on historical information that is relevant in today's world. For this reason I would like to acknowledge some of the people who inspired me to write these stories.

I would like to acknowledge the monumental efforts of Kerry R. Faunce as senior editor and publisher of our author website and our books. He has labored tirelessly over our manuscripts converting them into seamless finished and polished novels.

I would also like to praise and acknowledge Dr. Fran S. Watkins who has made many encouraging suggestions to improve the readability of all our efforts. She has been a taskmaster for the authenticity and facts of history gathered to support the plot line and continuity of the trilogy. These fictional stories and characters are based on real people and places, and in many cases real events.

Colonel David Hanson, who is a retired United States Army armored cavalry and military intelligence officer, has been a fantastic resource for these Chivalric Christian Orders' histories concerning many of the events in these novels.

Maura Basanty has been an encouraging voice contributing many ideas to improve and elucidate our efforts to bring our stories to fruition.

I would also like to acknowledge the ingenious creative abilities and suggestions of Mike McDowell in the creation of the illustrations and book covers for our books in this trilogy.

Respectfully,
Frank R. Faunce

CONTENTS

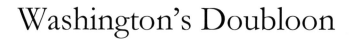

Washington's Doubloon

1 WASHINGTON'S SECRET LETTER

Everyone was enjoying their visit to Dr. Randall Fox's small Back Forty Ranch outside Salado, Texas. Doctors Carolyn and Christopher Rood had arrived earlier that morning from their home at Point Venture on Lake Travis north of Austin. Carolyn was inside the ranch house talking with Natalie von Shönfeld and Mary K. Stuart, Randall's next-door neighbor who looked after the ranch when he was away on one of his digs.

Randall and Christopher were sitting on the old-fashioned swing on the wide porch that covered the front of the ranch house. They sat in the swing perusing the countryside and discussing their individual research projects. Suddenly, Randall interrupted their discussions and related the latest news of a recent historical discovery given to the Department of History at the University of Texas.

"Yeah, the Department of History just acquired a hitherto unknown letter that Ephraim Brasher sent to George Washington in 1789 shortly after he became president of the United States on April 30, 1789. It seems a little strange to me that Brasher would send a letter to the president since he lived at 5 Cherry Street just next door to President Washington, who lived at 1 Cherry Street in New York City. Don't you think Brasher could just as easily walked over to his neighbor's house and told him what he had written?"

"Probably so, I would imagine," replied Christopher.

Randall continued, "You know, President Washington later the next year on November 27, 1790, moved to 524-30 Market Street in Philadelphia and lived there until he left office on March 10, 1797."

"I had forgotten that," replied Christopher.

Randall continued, "Yes, the new United States government that began in New York City picked up lock, stock and barrel and moved to Philadelphia in 1790."

He paused and then continued, "Yep, George and Martha, along with their whole household and household steward, Samuel Faunce, moved from New York to Philadelphia.

"Samuel Faunce, along with many of the founding fathers, was a fellow Scottish Rite Mason and a member of the exclusive Trinity Church. George Washington and his friends nicknamed Samuel Faunce *Blackie* because of his straight black hair. *Blackie* also had brilliant blue eyes and milky white skin as did most of his ancestors in New York and Plymouth, Massachusetts. His family was descended from John Faunce and Patience Morton who were Pilgrims who came from England to Plymouth in 1623 on the *Anne*, the second ship after the Mayflower.

"During his term in office as our first president, George Washington spent a great deal of his time overseeing the construction of the president's mansion, commonly called the White House, and the Capitol of Washington, D.C. The Capitol buildings were laid out in a grand design that George Washington personally approved. John Adams, though, was the first president to actually live in the White House. He moved into the White House in March 1797 before the plaster was even dry!"

Christopher impatiently asked, "So what was Brasher's letter about?"

"It wasn't about much really, just said something about a valuable gift he was giving George and to protect it," Randall explained. "It was the first golden doubloon struck by him personally as the designer of the first United States gold coin. Brasher even struck his initials on the national shield on the breast of the American eagle to authenticate it!

"The letter also mentioned something about protecting a valuable gift that had been given to the new nation that he referred to as the New Jerusalem on the Potomac. Then the letter mentioned something about their mutual friends and brother Masons, Alexander Hamilton and Major General Arthur Sinclair, who had been the fifteenth president of the Continental Congress in 1787 and first governor of the Old Northwest Territory."

"A valuable gift to the new nation?"

"The letter didn't say what that gift was," replied Randall.

Christopher grew silent and then replied, "Yes, I know General Sinclair was on Washington's staff during the Revolutionary War and the largest land owner in Western Pennsylvania." Then he paused and said, "You know he was at the Battle of Trenton when Washington crossed the Delaware River and devised the strategy that led to the capture of Princeton by Washington's forces. He was also with Washington as an aide de camp at Cornwallis's surrender of Yorktown. I believe he was born in Thurso, Scotland."

Then, Christopher mused, "He must have been related to Prince Henry Sinclair."

Randall replied, "Well as you know, Brasher was not only a lieutenant in the New York Militia, but also a Mason, a goldsmith, and a silversmith who made not only incidentals, but the state silverware Martha and George Washington used for their formal state dinners while he was President.

"He also knew Samuel Faunce whose family moved from the Lake Placid area of New York to Manhattan where he had an inn and tavern named after Charlotte, the wife of King George III. He also owned an entertainment park and a hotel. There was a portrait painting of Samuel when he was younger which showed him with a powdered wig, a fancy blue satin coat and breeches and flashing blue eyes and milky white skin. He must have been a quite wealthy dandy and a favorite of society in Manhattan. Nobody knew exactly where his wealth came from when he moved from Lake Placid."

That reminded Christopher of the relationship between the hidden part of the Knights Templar that called themselves the Fréré Maçons or Free Masons after the Inquisition of Friday, October 13, 1307, and the development of the "Enlightenment."

"You know, Randall, the whole thing that created this country and its concepts of freedom, the rights of the individual and the equality of everyone to pursue their dreams all started with the concept of Queen Margarette of Norway, Sweden, and Denmark and Prince Henry Sinclair of Orkney and their desire to create a New Jerusalem."

Randall interrupted, "Wait a minute. Isn't that what Brasher said? A New Jerusalem on the Potomac!"

"Yeah, you're correct," said Christopher. "Now, what were you saying?"

"I was going to ask what you think happened with all of that gold and silver treasure from the eighteen ships that left New Rochelle Harbor in 1307. You know the six ships that disappeared and the twelve ships that made it safely to Edinburgh were both carrying the Knights Templar belongings and treasure. The treasure was not at Saint Mary Chapel when we opened the secret chamber there."

They both knew from their last adventure that the gold and silver treasure from the twelve ships that was supposed to be hidden at Saint Mary Chapel was not there, but where had it gone? And what about Prince Henry's fleet with the Cistercian monks, select knights, and men at arms that had sailed for New Jerusalem in the spring of 1396 or his later voyage in 1398? They had supposedly left either on the earlier voyage or the later voyage with the treasure of the Knights Templar that was on the twelve ships anchored at La Rochelle that made it safely to Scotland and shelter. But, what happened to the other six ships that simply disappeared off the face of the earth?

Christopher mentioned that he and Carolyn had inherited Cliff House in Fairhope, Alabama, where they heard a legend about a Welsh Templar Knight, Prince Madoc ab Owain Gwynedd who sailed with a fleet of Welsh and Irish colonists from a port in Ireland to New Jerusalem. He landed in Mobile Bay under the cliffs of the Ecor Rouge, an early navigational marker and symbol used by the Aztec Indians and their allied tribes in the southeastern part of the United States. There is a history in the Cherokee Indian legends that spoke of a white tribe called the Welsh that battled with the Cherokees at Ohio Falls in the area of Louisville, Kentucky, Clark County, Indiana, and nearby Jeffersonville, Indiana, which was named after President Jefferson. Clarksville, Indiana, was where the Lewis and Clark Expedition had begun.

Thomas Jefferson by 1790 had heard about the Welsh white tribe from Gov. John Sevier of Tennessee who heard about the tribe from an elderly Cherokee Indian chief. John Sevier had later heard it from a Major Amos Stoddard in a letter dated August 30, 1810. Governor Sevier replied to this letter and said that in 1782 while on campaign against a part of the Cherokees, he met and became a friend of Chief Oconostota of the whole Cherokee Nation. The chief related that he had heard the story about the white Welsh tribe from his father and grandfather from legends told by their forebears about the Battle at the Ohio River Falls. He also related that the Welsh white tribe had crossed the Great Water (as the Indians called the Atlantic Ocean) and landed near the mouth of the Alabama River near Mobile Bay and had been driven north up the Alabama River to the Hiawassee River. He said the white Indians built stone forts as they moved north to the Ohio River Falls.

Christopher continued, "A man named John Brady in 1898 uncovered an ancient bronze helmet and shield on the Kentucky side of the Ohio Falls near a site where six and seven feet tall large sized skeletons were found in 1799 wearing brass breastplates adorned with the Welsh Coat of Arms. In the 1880s, thousands of skeletons were found in a meadow on the

Kelly farm outside Clarksville in Clark County, Indiana, on the other side of the Ohio River at the Ohio Falls area as if they had fallen in battle. Many of the bones were not Indian but were all of large stature just like the Indians had described the Welsh white tribe. Some of these skeletons were over seven feet tall, and one that was found in Columbus, Indiana, was almost eight feet tall!"

Randall looked surprised and said, "Wow, did anyone take any photographs of these skeletons?"

Christopher replied, "Yes, in the 1890s, and they still exist! Photographs were also taken in the 1890s of the skeletons, the brass and bronze helmets, shields, and breastplates found with the skeletons of the white Indians earlier in 1799, as well as the artifacts and skeletons found later in Kentucky and Indiana in the 1880s and 1890s.

"The Indian legends even spoke of a Welsh stone fort and walls on an island in the middle of the Ohio River just below the Ohio River Falls. Recent archeological excavations have found the foundations of such a fort on that island. The rest of the stones were carried off by settlers to build their houses and towns in the 1790s and 1800s. Remnants of the stone forts built from Mobile Bay to Indiana bear the same type of building design used by the Welsh, Scots, and Irish in the 1100s and 1300s."

Randall's eyes widened, and he said, "Maybe they were trying to reach the Great Lakes and the Saint Lawrence River Basin where earlier Viking explorers had been. Perhaps they thought they could find fellow Templars there since the Templars in the six ships that sailed to Mobile Bay to reinforce the settlements of Prince Madoc knew about the other ships that sailed on to Scotland and then to New Jerusalem in America."

"Probably," replied Christopher, "They usually had Cistercian monks with them who knew about the rüne stone markers with the hooked X. These markers have been found in Florida, Louisiana, Texas, Oklahoma, and at the juncture of the Mississippi River and the Missouri River, just like the ones found in Kensington, Minnesota, Iowa, New York, Massachusetts, and Nova Scotia."

He continued, "Maybe they planned to take the treasure from their six ships that landed at Mobile Bay and join it with the treasure that Prince Henry hid somewhere in Canada or New England. Maybe the Indian legends told by the Mi'qmaq, Mohican, and Mohawk tribes about a vast treasure brought by Prince Henry are true!"

Christopher stared at Randall and they simultaneously shouted, "We've got to find that treasure!"

2 THE BACK FORTY RANCH

"**B**oy is it hot for July," said Randall as he wiped the sweat from his brow. "I'm sure glad to see all of you. It's real nice to have some people and a beautiful young lady like Kira Ann around here, isn't it Mary K.?"

Mrs. Mary K. Stuart and Natalie von Schönfeld were just bringing a pitcher of lemonade and some glasses to Dr. Randall Fox, her husband, Dietrich and Dr. Christopher Rood who were sitting in three of the several rocking chairs lined up on the large front porch of the sprawling one-story ranch house that Randall called home. Mary Stuart was a widow and Randall's next-door neighbor down the road from the forty acres that Randall lovingly called his "Back Forty" Ranch.

Natalie was a startling beautiful young lady with a smooth milky complexion, tall, about five feet eight inches, slender with an athletic build like a professional dancer or athlete. She had dark brown almost black hair that tumbled around her shoulders like a halo. She had hazel eyes with blue speckles around the edges that gave her a dreamy look. She had a pleasant smile with a slight curl at the corners of her mouth revealing perfect white teeth that sparkled. She had the regal poise, calmness, and the persona of a queen who understood and loved her subjects. She was born and raised in the Czech Republic of Süd Deutsh parents and spoke seven languages perfectly without an accent. She had studied nursing with her friend, Rania, at the Karlova Medical Center in Prague.

She recently discovered from her mother that her maternal grandmother's parents were Askenazi Jews who had fled Germany to Czechoslovakia, became Catholics, and changed their names to hide their true identities after Adolf Hitler came to power. Many Jewish families such as American Secretary of State Madeleine Albright's parents had done the same thing to avoid the holocaust. She was an excellent skier and small boat sailor who had won many competitions in Czechoslovakia. She studied ballet and interpretive dancing where she excelled until she grew too tall and felt better suited for pediatric nursing. Her nature was studious and serious with a pleasant humor. She had met her husband Dietrich who was an officer and pilot in the German Luftwaffe while she was in Germany applying for a job at the Phillips University, Gnießen/Marburg Hospital.

Mary K. was a diminutive woman with dark hair and blue eyes who resembled the small painting of the "Mona Lisa" that Leonardo daVinci carried around with him during his lifetime. She was about five feet two inches tall with a slender build but carried herself as if she were much taller. She and her husband had befriended Dr. Fox long ago when he purchased the forty acres next to their larger ranch.

They had taken Randall under their wing and looked after his ranch as well as their own since he was away from home much of the time on his research, or "digs" as he called them. They paid him a small amount of annual rent money for the use of his forty acres as additional grazing land for their cattle. Sometimes they would use Randall's two-bedroom guest cottage that he had built for his three daughters and their families to use when they visited him. It was about fifty yards from Randall's ranch house.

"A comfortable distance," was how Randall put it. Randall

had a successful academic and research career in archeology and anthropology at the University of Texas in Austin. He had become a charming curmudgeon to his acquaintances and a loyal friend to those close to him and a stalwart defender and loving parent to his children. His adventures, digs, and lectures had taken him all over the world.

Natalie and Dietrich's six-year-old daughter, Kira Ann, who resembled her mother, had utterly charmed him. After he had found out that the Schönfelds were again being assigned to the German Luftwaffe Command in Texas and stationed at the Alamogordo Air Force Base in New Mexico, Randall impetuously bought a "painted" Shetland pony for Kira Ann for her birthday on June 24th. He purchased all the gear for the pony and even had a fancy stall and large tack locker built into his once empty barn. All of this without asking Natalie and Dietrich or even getting any advice from Mary K. Stuart.

The Stuarts had long looked after and maintained his ranch house, guest cottage, and land. Even after her husband's untimely accidental death, Mary K. had continued to look after his ranch.

When she found out about the visitation of the Schönfelds and the Roods, as well as the Shetland pony, she muttered to her ranch foreman, Jeremy, "I guess you better assign one of your cowhands the extra chore of taking care of "Daisy," the name she found that Kira Ann had picked out for the new mare. "And while you're at it, have him go over to Randall's ranch to help Natalie and Dietrich teach their six-year-going-on-twelve-year-old daughter how to feed, groom, ride, and generally take care of Daisy.

"Oh, also make sure there is plenty of feed and hay in the barn and have Doc Fischer give you the necessary medicines and tackle that will be necessary for that new locker in the barn."

Doc Fischer was an old family friend who liked to regale his friends with tales of the Old West he had heard from his grandfather.

Mary K. winked at Natalie as they put the lemonade and

glasses down on the small table next to the rocking chairs and said to Dietrich, Randall, and Christopher, "Matt, one of our ranch hands, will be coming over later this morning to help teach Kira how to ride and take care of her new pony."

No sooner had she mentioned Daisy, when a smiling Kira Ann came bouncing through the front door holding her hands up and excitedly announcing, "Mommy, Daddy, I'm going to ride my new horse this morning!"

Natalie corrected her, "One of Mrs. Stuart's cowboys, Matt, will be here soon to help Daddy and Uncle Randy—and she smiled at Randall as she said it—introduce you to your new pony, Daisy." She continued, "Daddy and his friends will teach you about how to ride and take care of your new friend."

"Oh, I know all about that. I've been reading all about horses—I mean ponies—and have been watching some old John Wayne cowboy movies that Uncle Randall has."

Dietrich, who was tall and handsome, stood up, scratched his blond head, looked at his wife, and winced his blue eyes as Natalie continued, "They will show you a little bit more so you will be comfortable taking care of your new friend."

Kira Ann looked up at her mother and said, "Can I get a cowgirl outfit?"

Natalie smiled at her daughter and softly said, "Yes, and with a cowgirl hat and boots."

Kira Ann waved at everyone and ran back inside the house to wait for Matt's arrival and to finish watching the old Betty Hutton movie, *Annie Get Your Gun,* that Randall had picked from his collection of old movie DVDs.

Carolyn, who was smaller than Natalie, had come out onto the porch to join everyone just as Kira had bolted through the front door to finish watching her movie. She waved at everyone and sat down with a glass of lemonade in her hand next to her husband, Christopher, who was slightly shorter than Dietrich but had the same blue eyes and blond hair as that of his cousins, the von Schönfelds. She laughed and said, "I see that you are all waiting for Matt to come over to help you teach Kira how to care for and ride her new pony. I think it's going to take a few days or maybe a week to teach her so she's comfortable with her new friend."

Mary K. agreed and said that when Natalie, Dietrich, and Kira returned to Alamogordo they would be glad to help them transfer the pony to the base's stables, or if they wished, they could keep Daisy here where she would be well taken care of and available whenever they visited the Roods. She explained that Matt would have the duty to care for their pony and be available any time they returned.

Natalie looked at Dietrich who said that it was up to Kira Ann and Natalie. Natalie smiled and replied, "I think we'll probably keep Daisy here until we return to Germany. That way, they will have an excuse to come back more often and visit with her cousins." She paused and looked at Mary K. and continued, "And visit with 'Uncle' Randall if he is around and not on one of his digs. You know how he likes to spin tall tales about cowboys and the old days."

Mary K. immediately replied, "Oh, don't worry about that. Matt will be available at any time, and the cottage and house will always be open for you. He likes to tell those yarns as well. It will be lovely to have a little girl to help look after since my daughter and her husband live so far away in Connecticut. I'm sure Randall would be okay with that."

She shifted her eyes hopefully to Randall who was sipping lazily on his lemonade.

Randall looked up and laconically replied, "Yep. That sounds good to me too."

Natalie and Dietrich smiled, looked at each other and winked. They almost simultaneously said, "Yep. That sounds good to us too." And then they all laughed.

About ten o'clock Matt drove up in his red Ford F-150 Raptor pickup truck with a horse trailer attached to it and parked it in the driveway in front of Randall's house. He waved at the people gathered on the front porch as he opened the door of the truck.

Kira Ann had finished her movie and was sitting beside her mother. She turned and looked at her mother and whispered,

"Is that the cowboy who is going to teach me all about riding Daisy?"

Natalie, replied, "I think so."

Matt got out of the truck and smiled at all of them, doffed his dove grey Stetson, and then put it on as Mary K. walked down the steps of the porch to meet him.

She shook Matt's hand and then turned and said to everyone, "I want you to meet our rodeo champion and best wrangler, Matt Johnson."

She introduced him to everyone and they all shook hands, even Kira Ann, who looked at his tanned face and asked, "Are you a real cowboy?"

"I shore am!" he replied. "Are you the little missy I'm going to teach how to take care of and ride her new pony?"

Kira Ann paused for a second, not quite understanding and then replied, "I shore am!"

Natalie cringed and then whispered to her daughter, "That's just Texan for I sure am." And she emphasized the word sure.

Kira Ann understood and smiled. They shook hands again and Matt took her hand and they all headed for the barn to meet Daisy.

Natalie and Mary decided to stay with Matt as he introduced Kira Ann to her new friend. Daisy looked at Kira and walked over to her as Kira Ann held her hand out to her. They looked at each other, Daisy licked Kira Ann's hand and Kira Ann put her arms around Daisy's neck, and their friendship began.

Everyone except Natalie and Dietrich left the barn at Matt's instructions while Kira and her parents became acquainted with Daisy. Matt had already been with Daisy for the week before, so she trusted him. Now it was time for the slow process of acquainting Daisy with her new friends.

Randall led everyone back to the porch and soon they were sitting in the rocking chairs chitchatting about what was happening with Randall and Christopher at the University of Texas and their research projects.

It didn't take long for Carolyn and Mary K. to excuse themselves and go inside the ranch house to clean up the morning's dishes and talk about what they were going to do over the next two weeks while Natalie and Dietrich were visiting. They had already planned to all have dinner at the Stagecoach Inn in Salado with Matt and discuss how Kira, Natalie, and Dietrich were getting along with Daisy.

3 THE QUEST BEGINS

As Christopher and Randall slumped back in their rocking chairs, they heard Matt, Natalie, Dietrich and Kira Ann closing the barn door and start walking toward the house. Kira Ann, immediately upon seeing her cousin Christopher and Uncle Randall, broke out into a run to the front steps, which she rapidly conquered, and jumped up into Christopher's waiting arms.

She breathlessly declared, "She likes me! She likes me! I even put a saddle on her and she let me get on it. She didn't even resist. When I got off, she licked my face!"

Her words tumbled all over themselves as she hugged her cousin and then kissed him on his cheek.

Randall whispered to Dietrich, "The games afoot, again. Christopher has found some clues to the missing Templar treasure! We'll tell you later all about what we have discovered."

Dietrich's eyes widened, and he muttered, "Really, you think you have found some clues?"

"Yes, really! But we'll discuss it later."

Dietrich was anxious to discover what they had been talking about, but he knew that this was not the time. The moment belonged to Kira Ann, and he knew that Natalie and Carolyn would not be in a mood to start talking about the possibility of resuming their search for the remainder of the Templar treasure.

Kira Ann turned to her mother and said, "May I ride Daisy later this afternoon?"

"Yes, I think that can be arranged. I'm so proud of you and I'm glad that Matt showed you how to put her reins and saddle on and take them off. Did you understand what he was saying about grooming her?"

"Yes, I believe she liked me brushing her." Then Kira Ann paused and said, "I think she liked the carrots and sugar. I do too!"

"Did you like watering her?"

"Yep!"

Natalie winced again and slowly said, "Yes, the word is yes."

"But, I want to sound like a Texas cowgirl!"

Natalie knew she was fighting a losing battle and replied, "We'll talk about that later. You know that Matt is also going to teach you how to train and show a pony as well as all the elements of riding and jumping. That will come later after he teaches you how to take care of Daisy, feed her, groom her, and bed her down for the night. It's all a lot of work."

"You mean it's just like taking care of a baby?"

"More like taking care of a six-year-old girl."

"Oh, I already know all about that," Kira Ann proffered.

Natalie hid her grin with her hand just as Dietrich came over and asked Kira Ann if she wanted to help Matt take his brown Quarter Horse, Tony, out of his trailer and put him in the stable with Daisy.

Kira Ann answered, "Yep!" and then corrected herself, "Yes, I didn't know Matt named his horse after Uncle Anton," and then she ran over to the trailer where Matt had already taken Tony out of the trailer and closed the door.

"What's with this 'Yep' business?" asked Dietrich.

"Well you know it's all about Texas, horses, and cowgirls," replied Natalie.

With that, she turned and walked over to Carolyn and Mary K. who had taken it all in and were covering their smiles with their hands.

"You heard all of that?"

They both said in unison, "Yep!" and then laughed.

Natalie sighed, "They grow up too fast, don't they?"

Mary K. shrugged her shoulders and replied, "Let's go inside and fix lunch before Randall decides he's going to fix it. You know he thinks he knows how to cook, but some of his concoctions would spoil our dinner tonight at the Stagecoach Inn."

The afternoon passed without incident and Kira Ann had an opportunity to not only ride Daisy alongside Matt and Tony, but also ride double on Tony. They didn't go far around the ranch, and when they got back to the barn, she enthusiastically joined in with Matt and Dietrich as they fed, watered, groomed, and dressed Daisy and Tony for the night.

Kira Ann thoroughly enjoyed her first day of being a cowgirl, especially after Randall presented her a cowgirl outfit complete with boots and a dove grey Texas Stetson hat.

Randall looked at her and then everyone and said, "She looks just like a Texas State Strutter!"

Everyone grinned, and Kira Ann looked up at her mother and whispered, "What is a Texas State Strutter?"

Natalie was lost for words, but Mary K. overheard the conversation and explained that the Texas State Strutters were an elite group of pretty girls at Texas State University who were female student dancers dressed in fancy cowgirl outfits who performed at Texas State athletic games and at special performances and events all over the United States.

Kira Ann looked at Mary K. and said, "Do they ride pretty horses?"

Mary K. replied, "I'm sure they do, but none as pretty as your Daisy."

Kira Ann seemed satisfied with that answer and then twirled around in her new outfit and asked, "Do I look as pretty as a Texas State Strutter?"

Matt spurted out, "You shore…," and then he looked at Mary K. and Natalie and continued, "Sure do!"

Natalie and Mary K. smiled back at him.

After dinner at the Stagecoach Inn in Salado, Mary K. and Matt drove back to Mary K's ranch, and Christopher drove everyone else back in his silver-grey Mercedes GLS class SUV to Randall's Back Forty Ranch and a good night's sleep.

The next morning, everyone was up early, but Mary K. was already in the kitchen preparing a good hearty Texas breakfast of ham, bacon, eggs, hashed browns, toast, orange and grapefruit juice, water melon, cantaloupe slices, and coffee with cream or milk. She had almost finished preparing breakfast when Carolyn, Kira Ann in her cowgirl outfit, and Natalie had arrived in the kitchen to help her finish the preparations. Matt had already left for the barn after he had finished his breakfast.

Natalie told everyone that Dietrich had been awakened by the smell of bacon and ham cooking and woke her up. Kira Ann was already dressed and patiently reading a book about riding a horse. She and Natalie met Carolyn in the hallway on their way to the kitchen.

Everyone else arrived about fifteen minutes later, but Randall was fast asleep, and Carolyn motioned to Christopher to go roust Randall out of bed. The two of them arrived about ten minutes later with Randall hastily dressed, unshaven, and his hair awry.

He apologized to everyone and slid into his chair at the head of the table, noting that Mary K. had already fixed his plate and everyone else except he and Christopher were halfway finished.

He remarked, "I know everyone is halfway around the track, but I'll catch up on the backstretch."

Mary K. frowned at him and Kira Ann looked bewildered.

Natalie leaned over to Kira Ann and said, "It's just a little joke about horse racing. Go ahead and finish your breakfast and then brush your teeth before you go out to the barn to see Matt, Daisy and Tony."

"Okay, Mommy."

It wasn't too long after this repartee and breakfast was finished that Dietrich cornered Christopher and Randall and asked about their conversation concerning the Templar treasure.

Christopher repeated the conversation and discussion that he and Randall had the day before. Dietrich listened spellbound and postulated that he believed their conclusions were correct, but where do they start?

Randall replied that the Mi'qmaq tribe still exists and maybe they should go to Nova Scotia to talk with the Mi'qmaqs and then look into talking with the Mohicans and the Mohawks about any specifics that they know.

Dietrich said to Christopher, "I'm going to have to obtain a couple weeks leave of absence from the base at Alamogordo before I can join you. When do you think you and Randall can get away from the University of Texas and go to Nova Scotia and New England?"

Christopher answered, "I'm not sure. I'll check with my secretary, Samantha Grünwald. How about you, Randall?"

"Oh, my slate is clean. I'm all caught up and could easily get away for a 'dig' anytime. My schedule is flexible. I'll check in with Dr. Allen Gaw and see what his schedule looks like. I think he would be a valuable asset since he is a linguist and understands many languages, especially some Indian languages. You know, Native American Indian culture and languages are his specialty. And besides, he's interested in the Templar treasure just like in Regensburg and Istanbul when we were looking for the Grail."

Dietrich replied, "Yeah, I remember." And then he laughed, "I just hope there aren't any bad guys like the Muslim Brotherhood in this caper."

As he said those words, he shuddered with a sense of foreboding, as if a cold breeze had brushed his shoulders. Little did he know what was in store for them.

Carolyn and Christopher had to leave and return to their house on Point Venture. He had to go to the medical center in San Antonio and check in with his research staff on a critical phase of their project on three-dimensional imaging of renal stones.

4 MYSTERY IN NOVA SCOTIA

It was about three o'clock in the morning the next day when Christopher received a telephone call from Randall. When Christopher answered the telephone, he spoke softly so as not to awaken Carolyn. He recognized Randall's voice. He sounded desperate.

"What's up, Randall?"

"You haven't heard?"

"Of course, I haven't heard. Carolyn and I have been asleep."

Carolyn rolled over toward her husband and said, "Not now. What does Randall want at this hour of the morning?"

"What do you want?"

"It's not what I want. It's what has happened. I just had a telephone call from Dr. Richards in Toronto. There were some killings and an attempted kidnapping of the chief of the Mi'qmaq tribe in Halifax, Nova Scotia."

"What is that all about and who is Dr. Richards?"

"You remember Mervyn Richards, don't you? He's the grand prior of the Hospitaller Order of Saint John in Canada. You know, the one who has the gorgeous wife with dark hair and blue eyes. Remember, her name is Betty?"

21

"Oh yeah, I remember. Mervyn's mother was Scottish and had migrated to Australia where Mervyn was born. He later immigrated to Canada, met Betty, and fell head over heels in love with her."

"Can you blame him? She was not only beautiful, but extremely intelligent."

"Yeah, I know. She told me that she has some Indian blood in her background—one of her ancestors married an Abenaki woman. Her family immigrated to Boston in 1638. There were two brothers whose last name was Jewett, I think. No, it was de Jouatt, and they were French Huguenots who later settled in Maine. One of the brothers, Betty's ancestor, married the daughter of an Eastern Abenaki chief. He was a Mi'qmaq!"

Randall paused to catch his breath. "You know, the tribe that adopted Prince Henry Sinclair into their tribe and called him Glooscap, a prince from the East who became a hero of Mi'qmaq tales and legends."

Randall then continued, "Earl Henry Sinclair, prince of Orkney, baron of Roslin and a vassal of Queen Margrette of Norway, Sweden, and Denmark was charged with the mission to fulfill the dream of Leif Erikson to create a new kingdom in Vinland."

Christopher replied, "Yeah, the Abenaki are one of the five Algonquin tribes that belonged to the Wabanaki Confederacy—the people of the dawn land. They were a confederation of five peaceful agrarian and hunting Canadian and American Indian tribes from Massachusetts to Nova Scotia that banded together for protection from the more aggressive Iroquois confederation. The Abenaki were a large tribe that had a western and an eastern component. The eastern component was the Mi'qmaq Indians that befriended Prince Henry's flotilla of ships that carried settlers, Cistercian priests from Göttland Island, soldiers and knights who carried the Knights Templar treasure from Saint Mary Chapel in Scotland to the *New Jerusalem* in the New World that Queen Margrette had envisioned to break the stranglehold the Hanseatic League had on northern maritime shipping of goods from the Silk

Route of China."

Randall broke in, "Yes, she certainly intended to create new trade routes to the colony of New Jerusalem which she and the Templars were going to create with the help the Abenaki tribes. Unfortunately, she was assassinated by agents of the Hanseatic League and her weakling son was subjected economically to the Hanseatic League's dictates. So, the settlers were abandoned, but not before they hid the Templar treasure somewhere."

"Queen Margrette," Christopher added, "had envisioned a colony that stretched from south of Hudson Bay at Kensington, Minnesota, along the 44th parallel to Oak Island in Nova Scotia, and from Kensington to the junction of the Missouri River and Mississippi River to its delta, and then east to Pensacola, Florida, and the eastern coast of America and Canada. Rüne stone markers have been found along those lines.

Randall did not answer, and all Christopher heard was a gentle sigh.

More silence and then Randall said, "I wonder why Dr. Richards and Betty are so concerned about the attempted kidnapping of the Indian chief?"

Carolyn, who had her ear pressed against the receiver of the telephone, chimed in, "Randall, why don't you call Mervyn and Betty back and ask them that question? Meanwhile, Christopher and I are going back to bed, and then later at a more reasonable time, fix breakfast and get ready for a new day. We can talk later. Okay?'

They agreed and both hung up.

Randall then called Mervyn and Betty and asked them about the significance of the attempted kidnapping.

Betty revealed that as a little girl, she had heard some of the legends and stories about Glooscap and about a huge treasure of silver and gold that Glooscap had brought along with his people from the land of the rising sun. They had come to show the Indians how to use strong metal knives, axes, and animal traps, how to increase the number of animal pelts. In exchange,

Glooscap would take their pelts back to the land of the sun. She said that she understood that only the chiefs over the centuries knew the secret of the vast treasure that Glooscap brought with him. She explained that the Indian legends were handed down over the centuries.

Mervyn added that the mayor of Halifax had just announced that three Indians were murdered by two Muslim Brotherhood jihadists when they tried to kidnap the chief of the tribe at gunpoint at a gathering of the tribal leaders of the Mi'qmaq Indian Tribe. Five other Indian Council members were slightly injured during the kidnapping attempt. The Indians subdued the terrorists and held them for the police until they arrived. The terrorists were from an ISIS faction of the Muslim Brotherhood and are now being questioned by the Canadian Security Intelligence Service, the CSIS.

Mervyn explained, "You know that Halifax is located on the undeeded lands of the Mi'qmaq Indians."

Randall sighed and then said, "I hope that I am going to be able to meet with the Mi'qmaq tribal leaders and the chief after this incident. What do you think?"

Mervyn replied, "I don't know what to think. Why would the Muslim Brotherhood want to kidnap the chief of the Mi'qmaqs? It doesn't make any sense."

With that, Randall agreed and told Mervyn and Betty that he would let them know what he learned after he flew to Halifax and sorted out the puzzle. They both hung up and Randall sat back in his chair next to the breakfast table in his kitchen and gazed at his now cold coffee and muttered to himself, "I better call Christopher and let him know what I have had found out about the Halifax affair." But not until he got a new cup of coffee.

Randall then called Christopher back, and a sleepy voice answered the phone, "Hi, Randall, what's up?"

Randall relayed the information he had gotten from Betty and Mervyn and apologized for the late hour.

Christopher replied, "Let's meet for lunch tomorrow. Call Samantha at my office and set up a meeting. Okay?"

"Yeah, I'll call Sam. Good night—sorry for the late hour."
Then he hung up.

Christopher stared at the empty ceiling, and Carolyn asked him what he was looking at.

Christopher replied, "I don't know. I guess I'm searching for a vision. I'll tell you in the morning."

Carolyn rolled over, kissed him, and softly said, "Okay."

It didn't take long before the morning sun was rising and shining into Carolyn and Christopher's bedroom window. Christopher had a difficult time sleeping after Randall's telephone call and welcomed the morning sun. He knew that a critical time in his research at the university had arrived, and that he probably couldn't go to Nova Scotia with Randall.

He turned over to kiss Carolyn as she stirred, rubbed her eyes, and looked at Christopher. They kissed, and Christopher murmured, "I don't think I'm going to be able to go to Halifax. We are at a point in our research where I just have to be here."

"Just as well. It sounds dangerous, and I'm sure the police can handle everything," Carolyn replied.

"I know, but I hate to miss the action."

"You said the same thing when you left for Desert Storm, remember?"

Christopher hung his head down and murmured, "Yeah, I know."

Carolyn reached over and patted him softly on the shoulder as she got out of bed and said, "Let's get a cup of coffee and have some breakfast before you call Randall back and tell him you can't go with him and Allen."

Half an hour later, Christopher called Randall and explained that he couldn't get away because he was at a critical phase in his research and just couldn't leave.

Randall replied that he understood and said that it was okay, and that Allen had told him he was free and would be able to get away from the University of Texas for a while. He was going to take his daughter, Lauren, who is visiting with him, when they all go to Halifax. She just finished a movie in Hollywood and was now between "gigs."

Allen's daughter is an accomplished actress who lives in Pacific Palisades, California, and loves to occasionally take her Sun Odessey 54 DS sailboat, berthed at Marina del Rey in Los Angeles, out into the Catalina Channel for an afternoon of relaxation. She is always interested in accompanying her father when he is on a dig or solving a mystery.

Lauren Gaw is a beautiful young lady who is about five feet two inches tall and has a Black Belt in Karate and the martial arts. She has long black hair and an athletic body from her training as a dancer and champion gymnast. She speaks several languages and is an accomplished sailor like Natalie. From her study of psychology, human behavior, and acting, she is proficient in nonverbal communication and various nuances of posture and body language to detect the innermost thoughts of people. Her father believes her to be a "mind reader" because she can complete his sentences almost before he speaks them. She seems to have the skill to be two steps ahead of everyone. She loves puzzles and mysteries. She is also well-read on history, architecture, and design.

It was a day later when Allen and Lauren arrived at the Back Forty Ranch. He and Lauren had driven from his Frank Lloyd Wright house on Point Venture. The sun was just beginning to set when they arrived, and Randall had Allen's Glenlivet Scotch and soda ready for him when they arrived. Lauren preferred some Perrier with a twist of lime. She smiled at Randall, Natalie, Dietrich, Matt, Mary K., and Kira Ann who, with Matt's help, had just finishing bedding down Daisy.

Kira Ann ran up to Allen and Lauren and said to them, "Do you like ice cream like cousin Christopher?"

Allen had already been clued in by Natalie and Dietrich from their last adventure with the Seton Secret that Kira Ann loved ice cream and wasn't shy about enlisting the aid of friends who might also like ice cream to get an extra helping at dinner.

Lauren smiled and looked at Natalie, who nodded her head, as she picked up Kira Ann and hugged her, then let her down as she winked at her and said, "I do!"

Kira Ann squeezed Lauren's hand and said with an impish smile, "Me too!"

Mary K. looked amused at this interplay and announced that dinner would soon be ready after everyone had an opportunity to relax for a few minutes and enjoy their reunion and meeting Lauren. Then she smiled broadly at Kira Ann and Lauren and said they had plenty of ice cream of a variety of flavors.

Kira Ann immediately announced that she liked Neapolitan ice cream best because it had three flavors.

Lauren looked at Kira Ann and said enthusiastically, "Me too!"

5 WHAT TO DO?

After dinner, Natalie and Dietrich asked Kira if she wanted to watch television or read one of her books of poetry that Rania had given her.

Kira Ann said that she didn't know if she wanted to read the Zane Grey Westerns now that she was a cowgirl or read the poetry of James Whitcomb Riley, the Hoosier poet. She giggled, then said she liked James Whitcomb Riley because his poems were so funny, and then she looked at her father and asked, "What does Hoosier mean."

Dietrich thought for a minute, wrinkled his eyebrows, shrugged his shoulders in despair and replied, "I don't know." Then he looked toward Natalie and smiled knowingly, "Nobody knows for sure. It's a mystery to even the citizens of Indiana who call themselves Hoosiers."

Kira smiled and proclaimed that she loves mysteries. She then suddenly blurted out, "I think I'll read a Zane Grey mystery since I'm going to be a Texas State Strutter someday."

Dietrich stammered, "Where did she get that notion?"

Then he glanced at Natalie who shifted her eyes toward Randall who had a sheepish look on his face.

"I might have known," Dietrich exclaimed.

Lauren and Allen grinned at each other, and then Lauren asked, "Dad, what do you know about the Mi'qmaq chief or what he might know that made those terrorists want to kidnap him?"

Allen replied, "There's a legend among the tribe that has been handed down for centuries that when Glooscap, or rather Prince Henry Sinclair, sailed south with the treasure and his flotilla, he confided to his blood brother, the chief of the tribe and only to be known by subsequent chiefs where he was going. To this day, only the chiefs of the tribe have had this secret handed down to them through the centuries. The Mi'qmaq's are known for their honesty and trustworthiness. The legend was that the flotilla sailed south leaving clues along the way."

Allen continued as everyone listened with rapt attention, "Among those possible clues are the Oak Island mystery, the Westford boat stone, the Westford, Massachusetts, Knight and sword carving, the Tyngsboro map stone near the Merrimack River in Massachusetts, the Narragansett Rüne Stone, and the Newport, Road Island, Stone Tower with its Venus windows. All are supposed to be clues from the voyages of Prince Henry Sinclair with Antonio Zeno from Venice as his navigator. The Nicolo and Antonio Zeno narratives and maps archived in Venice can be used to authenticate Prince Henry's voyages to New Jerusalem following the voyages of Leif Erikson to the New World and Vinland, which Prince Henry and Queen Margarette called the New Jerusalem. No one to date has been able to figure out the location of the fabulous Templar treasure that once resided in Scotland."

He continued, "Even George Washington and Franklin Delano Roosevelt became involved in the mystery and search for treasure on Oak Island. I believe these Muslim Brotherhood terrorists who tried to kidnap the chief of the Mi'gmaqs were interested in kidnapping and forcing the chief to divulge the ancient secret of Glooscap! I think when I have a chance to speak with the chief in his own language I may be able to gather some more information that might shed some light on this ancient mystery."

Everyone, except Kira Ann who had withdrawn to one of Randall's comfortable leather chairs on the other side of his living room to read her book, was enraptured as Allen continued his narrative and explained what he knew about the keys or clues left behind by Prince Henry and his expedition.

Lauren was particularly interested in the Venus windows of the Newport Tower and pressed her father on the symbolism of the Knights Templar and their devotion to the sacred feminine. She was particularly interested when he explained the peculiarity of the hooked X that was unique to these marker rüne stones that marked the boundaries of the lost colony of New Jerusalem.

Allen explained that the X was not a real X, but was a chalice symbol on top of a phallus symbol and the chalice, or upper part of the X, had a small diagonal line emanating on the right inside arm of the upper part of the X. Some have claimed that the upper part of the X represented Mary Magdalene with the small spur representing a child.

It is known that many of the members of the original Knights Templar were Cathar Christians who worshipped Mary Magdalene as the favorite apostle of Christ as is mentioned in the Gospel of Thomas found in the Nag Hammadi Gnostic scrolls.

He explained that this unique X was only used by the Cistercian Monks from Göttland Island whose chapel construction on the island resembles the construction techniques used in the late 1300s to build the Newport Tower in Newport, Rhode Island. The 44th parallel apparently is the uppermost border of New Jerusalem marked by the Kensington rüne stone in Minnesota and the marker on Oak Island, Nova Scotia! The Cistercian Monks were called the White Friars because of their white frocks, same as the Knights Templar. The Knights Templar were founded by Saint Bernard who was the leader of the Cistercian Order and wrote the Benedictine Rule or Law for both orders.

Dietrich asked, "If the chiefs know where the treasure is

hidden or know clues that would reveal the location, why haven't they recovered the treasure?"

Allen replied, "The Abenaki chiefs declare they are children of the earth and sky and put more value in preserving the earth and its environs than they do the evil that money brings."

Dietrich smiled and quipped, "Do the tribe members know that?"

Allen laughed and replied, "I think so."

Lauren was taking this all in and declared that she thought the symbols to which the Knights Templar were addicted probably were more apparent than we imagine and that many times we look for answers to riddles that are more complicated than need be. Sometimes solutions are simple, and we overlook them. She then cited the legend of the puzzle of the Phrygian Gordian Knot and its prophecy which Alexander the Great promptly solved and then conquered Asia.

"Sometimes," she said, "The solution is right in front of us and we don't recognize it!"

Little did they know that she would be correct. The pieces of the puzzle were directly in the narrative laid out by her father.

Allen then suggested that before they all went up to Halifax, perhaps it would be better if only Randall, Lauren and he go to Halifax to get the facts and then come back and lay them before everyone to carefully examine.

Natalie and Dietrich promptly agreed. After all, he still had not gotten his leave of absence and besides, Randall, Allen, and Lauren were already on holiday or leave of absence and did not have to wait for permissions.

That was it! They all breathed a sigh of relief, and Allen broke the tension by saying to his old friend, "Randall, since you taught me how to drink single malt Scotch years ago when we had a similar, no pun intended, knotty research problem to solve, let's break out your Glenlivet Scotch and relax."

They all wholeheartedly agreed.

6 HALIFAX

The intrepid trio of researchers or more correctly, detectives, arrived two days later ready and eager for their flight to New York and then Halifax, Nova Scotia. The weather was clear and sunny on this particular spring day in April, but they knew it would still be nippy in Canada. They had packed their winter coats just in case a Norther would blow in from the Arctic. It had been recorded that Prince Henry had arrived in the New World on the 28th of May 1396, so they felt that spring would be a good time to arrive in Halifax, even though it was the 28th of April.

They departed Austin-Bergstrom Airport exactly on time and had no difficulty catching their connecting flight to Halifax from New York. Miraculously, the flight into JFK airport was on time, and thirty minutes later they were on board their flight to Halifax International airport without a hitch. They cleared passport control and customs smoothly and reached the Prince George Hotel in downtown Halifax without a hitch by taxi. They had booked suites next to each other, convenient for conferencing.

The chief of the Mi'qmaq Indian Grand Council was unable to tell Allen anything about any secrets passed down from chief to chief, and no one in the Grand Council would talk about the terrorist attack on them. It was as if nothing had happened, and everywhere they turned there was silence. Lauren had noted, however, that the white flag of the Mi'qmaq tribe had a red Templar cross with a red star and a red crescent on either side of the horizontal arms of the cross.

While they were there, Randall called Mervyn and Betty and told them about meeting with the chief and the Mi'qmaq Grand Council. Betty replied that they were probably afraid of saying anything because of the ongoing investigation by the CSIS, the Canadian Security Intelligence Service.

Randall then asked Betty if she knew anything about the secret the chiefs of the tribe only knew.

Betty paused and then said, "I only know what has been passed down through my family from the time my ancestor married the chief's daughter. She supposedly told her husband that the path to the treasure would only be revealed by the Venus window at the time of the harvest moon, but she did not elaborate on anything else because of her fear for her life if she said more."

Randall thanked his old friends and they said their goodbyes. Betty said she was sorry they couldn't be of any more help and that they had been on a wild goose chase in Halifax.

After the telephone conversation ended, Lauren sat in her chair very quietly while she pondered what she had just heard. Suddenly she stood up and excitedly said, "Yes, it's so simple! The key word is path. But what does that relate to? Prince Henry was sailing somewhere. It doesn't have anything to do with a land path—it means a sailing route, but where? Dad, where did Prince Henry sail?"

Allen looked at his daughter and realized she had stumbled onto something like the Gordian knot puzzle of Alexander the Great. As he was looking at Lauren, she suddenly burst out and said, "The solution is so simple—we are looking straight at it, but where is the lynchpin?"

Randall muttered, "Lynchpin. What does that mean?"

Lauren excitedly replied, "The key—something that holds parts together."

"Dad, you're right. All Alexander did was to remove the lynchpin from the middle of the knot in the rope that secured the wagon. All we have to do is find the wagon. It's something that Prince Henry left for everyone to see that he knew would not disappear with time."

Randall declared, "Then we are in the wrong place. The terrorists don't realize that the chief doesn't know where the treasure is—he only knows indirectly about the means of finding the clue leading to the treasure! It's like the two key locks on the treasure boxes used by the Spanish in their treasure galleons. It takes two keys to unlock the two locks on the boxes."

Lauren finished his sentence, "It takes two keys simultaneously to unlock the clue to the path of the treasure!"

Allen looked at his daughter with pride and inwardly said to himself, "It might be a three lock and key puzzle!"

The three adventurers sat down silently and then Lauren reached for the glass with the Glenlivet Scotch that her father had just poured for the three of them. They touched their glasses together and Allen said, "Just like the three musketeers!" And then they all laughed.

The next day they were on their way back to Austin and then the Back Forty Ranch to fill in the blanks for Natalie and Dietrich.

After explaining everything to them, Allen commented, "We better fill in Carolyn and Christopher. He'll be happy to find out there was no action, and Carolyn will be happy there was no danger that her husband might have encountered."

After arriving at the ranch, Lauren went over to Kira Ann who was working one of Randall's jig saw puzzles to see how she was doing.

Kira Ann looked up and said, "Uncle Randall got me a more difficult puzzle than the last one."

Lauren sat down beside her and said, "Let's just see how difficult Uncle Randall's puzzle is."

Allen motioned to his comrades and said, "That's my Lauren. She has always had a knack for solving puzzles and has developed a sixth sense about them."

Randall looked over at his old friend and noticed the pride on his face as he watched his daughter working patiently on the puzzle with Kira Ann. Then he looked around and saw the same look on the faces of Natalie and Dietrich as they watched their precocious daughter interacting with Lauren.

Randall's mind wandered back in time when his own daughters were children and he really missed those days. He took a deep breath and fought back the moisture that was building in his eyes. He felt like Rip Van Winkle who had awakened in the wrong century.

7 DANGER STRIKES!

Dietrich had just received his leave of absence for a month from the Luftwaffe. He was finishing his breakfast in the kitchen of his house in Alamogordo, New Mexico, when Natalie entered their kitchen after checking on Kira Ann. She told her husband that Kira Ann was busily brushing her teeth after she had finished her breakfast.

"Well, that's done. She's going to play in the backyard for a while. She misses Daisy. I told her that Randall will ship her to us when we are done with our mystery. She acts so grown up. She says she can stay with Mary K. and Matt if we have to go somewhere on our adventure. I believe that she really likes the idea of being a cowgirl and taking care of her pony."

Dietrich quipped, "I guess it's just that mother instinct that you ladies have."

Natalie couldn't let that pass and smiled as she replied, "Yes and it's a good thing that you were raised with both of your parents, so your mother could give you a good dose of common sense. I shudder to think what the world would be like if only men controlled everything!"

She suddenly realized what she had said and that in many parts of the world, women did not live with equal status in their families or their society. She looked at Dietrich and said, "I guess it's easy for all of us to forget how lucky we are to live in a society in the Western world where the equality of all humans and their rights are cherished and defended!"

Kira Ann burst into the kitchen and proclaimed that she had brushed her teeth, gums, tongue, and everything and was now ready to go outside and tend to her flower garden that she and her mother had planted. She ran over to her father, smiled and said, "Daddy, see how pretty my teeth look!"

Dietrich picked her up and kissed her and then put her down on the floor. Kira Ann turned to her mother and asked her if she would come out in the garden to help her trim the roses. Natalie reminded her to wear her gloves because of the thorns.

Kira replied as she held up her gloves, "Mommy, see I have them right here," and then ran over and kissed her mother as Natalie leaned down to receive her morning salute.

Natalie poured herself a cup of coffee with cream and looked at the morning paper that Dietrich had laid on an empty chair. As she was perusing the headlines, she noticed a headline that spoke of a family in the Miami, Florida, area being robbed at gunpoint during a house break in. She softly said to Dietrich, "I can't believe how brazen these crooks are nowadays."

Dietrich looked up from his scrambled eggs and said, "What are you talking about?"

Natalie replied as she read from the newspaper, "It says here that their house was broken into shortly after dawn when the husband turned off the house alarm system to go outside to pick up the morning newspaper. The gang of three young black men and one white woman with ski masks rushed him with drawn pistols and a knife and forced him back into his house where they tied up his wife, teenaged son, and young daughter with duct tape and gagged them. After threatening his wife and children and then beating up his teenaged son and breaking his arm after he refused to cooperate, he was forced to open his home safe that was hidden behind a bookcase and give them a precious collector's gold coin. They didn't take any of the jewelry or cash that was also in the safe."

"That's odd," Dietrich replied, "I wonder why the crooks didn't take the cash or jewelry. It doesn't make any sense."

Natalie continued, "It says that the three were apprehended within an hour when the three crooks stopped at an emergency clinic to get some care for one of the young men who had a cut on his leg that was bleeding. When the young man was taken alone back to a treatment room to clean, stitch and dress the wound, he had to take his pants off and the nurse noticed a piece of duct tape on the young man's ankle. As the doctor was tending the wound, the nurse removed the duct tape despite the young man's resistance to her doing so. Two orderlies grabbed the patient and that's when the nurse saw the stolen gold coin stuck on the tape. The doctor suspected something was wrong and had the nurse call the police. The police arrived and arrested the two unsuspecting men and woman in the reception room of the clinic and the patient who was being treated."

"Amazing!" muttered Dietrich.

Natalie read on, "Apparently, the young black man with the cut had sustained the wound to his leg in his struggle with their victim's teenaged son while he was being subdued."

"Who were the three men and the woman?"

Natalie continued, "They were later identified as members of a Muslim Brotherhood faction being protected by a mosque in a Miami suburb."

With that, Dietrich sat up straight in his chair and exclaimed, "Have they identified the coin they stole?"

"Yes, it says here that it is a rare gold coin of which there are only seven in existence in the world today, and that was sold by the Yale University Library several years ago to the wealthy man from whom they stole it."

"Did they say what the coin was?" Dietrich asked.

Natalie looked up from the newspaper and said to Dietrich, "Leibchen, it's the coin all of you have been looking for. It's a Brasher Doubloon!"

Dietrich thought for a minute and then he sighed in relief

and said, "No, it's not the one. The Brotherhood doesn't know about Washington's Doubloon. They think that any of the doubloons will reveal the secret, and I just realized why Ephraim Brasher sent a letter to George Washington when all he had to do was walk down the street to Washington's house on Cherry Street in New York when they were next door neighbors. There is something about the doubloon that he personally made only for George Washington. The Washington Doubloon is the most expensive of the remaining Brasher Doubloons!"

Natalie's eyes widened in disbelief that a single coin could be worth a fortune. She asked her husband, "How much is the Washington Doubloon worth?"

Dietrich grinned as he looked at his wife, "Take a deep breath and hold still. The last time it was sold, it was worth over $7.4 million!"

Natalie gasped, "We can't buy it! Why do you, Randall, and Christopher want it?"

Dietrich smiled, got up from his chair, walked over to Natalie, and leaned down and kissed her on her cheek as he whispered, "We don't want to buy it, we just want to see it and examine it to see what is so special about it that Ephraim Brasher had to write a secret down in a letter rather than just tell his friend, neighbor, and fellow Mason, George Washington!"

"Oh, that's all. What makes you think the owner of that particular coin will let you look at it?"

Dietrich sat back down in his chair, drank his coffee, and almost whispered, "You're correct. He, or rather the corporation, might not."

Dietrich elaborated, "Blanchard and Company, the New Orleans-based coin and precious metals company brokered the deal and said that the doubloon was purchased by an undisclosed Wall Street investment firm. The identity of the seller and buyer was not disclosed."

He explained to Natalie that the coin contains 26.66 grams of gold, which is slightly less than an ounce. The coin was worth about $15 when it was minted, and the gold value would be slightly more than $1,500 today.

8 WHAT'S SO SPECIAL?

Dietrich called Randall and told him the story about the robbery in Miami that Natalie had read to him. Randall was surprised over the amateurish nature of the robbery and told Dietrich that if they had taken the jewelry and cash as well as the coin, the police would be thinking that it was just a foiled robbery by some misguided young people rather than a worldwide organization like the Muslim Brotherhood. This now brings into play the international community and the FBI, the CIA, the CSIS, MI5 and the Mossad, not to mention Interpol.

Dietrich commented further that the three individuals arrested had also been part-time actors in bit parts in Hollywood and New York, and the young lady involved in the crime had also done some modeling for advertisements.

Now, all these agencies will be asking questions about the Brotherhood's activities and what does it have to do with the black community or the American entertainment community.

When Randall contacted Allen and told him about the attempted robbery, he said it also would be tied to the murders and assault on the Mi'qmaq Indians in Halifax. Allen said Lauren was concerned about possible connections within the various actors' groups. She mentioned that most actors were generous and well-intentioned but might be too naive when it came to international organizations like the Muslim Brotherhood.

Allen and Lauren decided they needed to get together with Randall and discuss the situation that now presented itself. When they arrived at the Back Forty Ranch, they were surprised to see that Christopher was already there and wanted to know what he thought about the situation.

Allen remarked, "Lauren and I didn't expect you since we knew you were tied up in a critical phase of your research, and since we are neighbors on Point Venture, we could have all come together in my car."

Christopher apologized and said he was sorry, but the story of the robbery in Miami had shaken him so that he knew he needed to get with everyone to discuss what was different between Washington's Doubloon and all the other doubloons.

Christopher related that he thought there must be some metallurgical difference in the gold used for the Washington Doubloon and spoke about the differences in the gold alloy used for that specific coin that might reveal something. He mentioned a color metallography technique that had been developed by Dr. E. Beraha and B. Shpigler which can determine slight color differences in the metallic grain structure of a coin that could not be seen under normal lighting circumstances.

Lauren pointed out these techniques had been developed in the 1970s and would not have been available in colonial times.

Christopher then mentioned Egyptian Blue pigmentation that had been used in ancient times for invisible cryptography to reveal secret information on metals that could be seen under certain red-light sources. They all agreed that might have some validity since the Frérè Maçon certainly knew about Egyptian Blue. But the rub was getting the corporation that now owns the Washington Doubloon to allow them not only to see the doubloon, but to actually handle it and expose it to the red light that might reveal any secrets.

Christopher glanced around the group and then chuckled, "Well, not to sound corny, that's a horse of a different color."

Everyone laughed, and Randall said, "Well, if we can find out who the actual owner is, it's worth a try. All they can say is no!"

Then he added, "I don't think this latest robbery attempt is going to make it any easier for us to have the opportunity to actually see it."

Lauren piped in and said, "Maybe we are looking at this thing wrong. Maybe a high definition photograph would suffice without actually seeing it. If a photograph taken under the proper red light were used, could it show anything?"

Christopher wrinkled his eyebrow and said, "Perhaps. It's worth a shot, but I think Randall is right. It's going to be difficult if not impossible to find out who bought it and then get their permission to photograph it under the proper lighting conditions."

Lauren then added, "To paraphrase Shakespeare, *the fault is not within the stars, but rather is within us.* I think we are trying to make this too difficult. Maybe we should try to find out what was in the letter that Ephraim Brasher gave to George Washington. Does anyone know what happened to it?"

"That may be difficult," Allen remarked. "Martha Washington burned most of George's personal correspondence after he died, and the rest would have been passed down to their heirs. Some may be in a museum or in a chest in someone's attic."

Lauren mused, "What was it Randall said about the expedition of Prince Henry and Antonio Zeno? Weren't the Zeno brothers navigators who used the stars and the astrolabe for navigation? Didn't he say that the Mi'qmaqs referred to the flotilla as the people of the Dawn Land? Maybe the important clue is in the path the expedition took after they left Nova Scotia and the territory of the Abenaki? Maybe we would be better served to try and determine their route and where they sailed to?"

Christopher said he thought he better get back to San

43

Antonio and his research team and make sure everything was okay there. He said he was very sorry that he had to leave the Back Forty Ranch but would keep in touch with them. He thanked everyone for letting him know about the developments that have occurred and to let him know if anything new developed. He shook their hands and then left for San Antonio.

Mary K. and Matt arrived at the ranch and she noted that she had extra guests for dinner. After greeting everyone she went to the kitchen to start preparing the grub, as she referred to the dinner meal. She had planned on serving steak and hash brown potatoes with a salad, but wasn't sure Randall had enough for everyone, so she prepared a list of things she needed for the meal. She asked Matt to go back to her ranch and fetch the items on her list. The list was not long, and Matt willingly departed to get what Mary K. wanted. He was uncomfortable around such high falutin' company.

Mary K. went to the guest rooms to make sure all their beds were made and ready for the night. The weather was clear and warm for the late spring and the weatherman had said there might be some good Lyrid meteor showers later in the evening and night. When Mary K. went back to Randall's large ranch house living room, he had already brought out the liquor and was asking everyone what they wanted before dinner. He joked that he was not going to be like Ida Wilson, a famous hostess and multimillionaire from Corpus Christi who frequently declared that her guests could have any drink they wanted as long as it was bourbon and branch. In his youth, he had attended a few of her gala soirees.

He said he had a few wines, and Lauren opted for a nice California Merlot since Mary K. was preparing filet mignon steaks and Texas style barbecued ribs, all prepared over a mesquite grill.

Everyone else had some Glenlivet Scotch to help whet their appetites.

The dinner went well, and Matt had finally warmed up and explained that the large front porch was a fine place to watch the meteor showers in the unusually dark night sky. The country air was refreshing, and Lauren told everyone that she had almost forgotten how pleasant it was to be able to enjoy the pleasant fresh air of the country and see the stars at night. She said it was impossible to enjoy the night in Hollywood because of the haze and bright lights. She said she remembered how it was when she was a little girl, and her father and mother used to camp out under the stars in Texas. She added that she was fond of night sailing off the coast of California just like when she was learning how to sail in the Gulf waters off the coast of Galveston.

Randall mentioned that Natalie and Dietrich were also excellent sailors and wished they and Kira Ann were with them. He also mentioned that he too used to sail in the Gulf when he was younger.

Mary K. said that she too wished everyone could be there to witness the meteor showers that were particularly spectacular that night.

Matt, upon hearing that, joined in and declared, "I shore do wish that Missy Kira Ann were here with her parents to see all of this."

They all laughed, and Allen mischievously chimed in, "I certainly shore do too!"

Lauren gently elbowed her father in the ribs and whispered to him, "Don't make fun—it's not nice!"

Allen turned to his daughter, smiled and whispered back, "Yes ma'am."

9 A BREAK IN THE CLOUDS

The sun was breaking through the overcast morning sky and illuminating the reddish face of the Sea Cliff of the Ecor Rouge, a landmark of Fairhope, Alabama, that was used for navigational purposes by the Aztecs and the ships of the Vikings and later Spanish explorers. Donnie Barrett, the museum director at the Fairhope Museum of History, had shown Carolyn and Christopher early photographs of the Ecor Rouge glistening in the sunlight. The same sun that had illuminated the ancient sea cliffs now was shining through the large bayside master bedroom windows looking out onto the expansive front porch of Cliff House, the retreat home of Carolyn and Christopher Rood.

The house was located next to a large well-kept park filled with flower gardens and southern oak trees dripping with Spanish moss that gave an ethereal panorama feeling of the Antebellum South. The park and lawn of Cliff House lay atop a cliff that overlooked a white sand beach and the expanse of Mobile Bay. Carolyn had hung multiple flower vases from the ceiling of the porch that ran the breadth of the house. The multicolored flowers and green fern pots were gently swaying in the soft sea breeze that filled the porch.

Carolyn and Christopher had retreated for a much-needed rest from their house at Point Venture at Lake Travis after Christopher had successfully completed the research project at The University of Texas Medical School in San Antonio. They had inherited the house and some property from Carolyn's close cousin and she had turned it into a garden house with a grand view of the bay and Ecor Rouge. The seagulls and pelicans were coasting on the gentle sea breeze looking for fish that had wandered too close to the surface.

Carolyn has been up early to fix a breakfast of orange juice, fresh fruit, toast and honey, a poached egg, and a carafe of French roast coffee. Christopher had stumbled late out of bed and, after shaving and showering, wandered into the breakfast room. He was dressed casually as was Carolyn, and she had poured a cup of coffee for him when she heard him shuffling down the ceramic floored hall toward the breakfast room.

She gently kissed him as he came through the door and handed him his cup of coffee with cream.

"Good morning," she said as he came through the door. "Did you get enough sleep?"

He looked lovingly at her and said, "Yes, and it really felt good after these hectic last two weeks at the research center. How about you?"

"Yes, I feel good. What's on the agenda for today? Are you going to check out our boat, take some pictures of the oak trees, flowers or, then she slipped it in, the rüne stones?"

Her question startled him because he had not thought of their Templar quest since their meetings at the Back Forty Ranch.

He thought for a minute and then said, "Carolyn, we've looked at the rüne stones and fragments of stone buildings and walls around here and they seem similar to the stone walls and structures built by Prince Madoc and his Welch and Irish settlers in the Southern and Midwestern states as a part of the Templar's early settlement of New Jerusalem. What do you think?"

She smiled and said, "I thought that was what you were

thinking about. Yes, they do seem similar."

Christopher looked at Carolyn and continued, "Prince Madoc ab Owain Gwynedd was, according to some accounts, a Templar knight who sailed to Mobile Bay in America in 1170 as part of the Scandinavian settlements of the Vikings, such as those discovered in Vinland, Greenland, and Iceland. Those Vikings were from Norway, Sweden, and Denmark that Queen Margarette later ruled."

"Yes," Carolyn replied, "And legend also tells us that the six missing ships from the Templar fleet that sailed from La Rochelle harbor on the early morning hours of Friday, October 13th, 1307, sailed to reinforce Prince Madoc's settlement at Fairhope while the other twelve ships sailed to Scotland for refuge."

Christopher nodded his head and said, "Those settlers at Fairhope probably later built the stone towers and forts found in the Southern and Midwest states of America."

He expanded on his theory, "There is even evidence that the early Viking explorers sailed as far as the Aztec kingdom and left rüne stones and noted natural navigational markers such as the Ecor Rouge to aid their later expeditions. They also built stone towers like the one in Newport, Rhode Island, to aid them in their voyages and explorations of the North American continent. The stone constructions and towers in New England and from here to Lookout Mountain and Louisville probably helped guide their internal exploration of North America."

Christopher sheepishly looked at Carolyn and said, "How about if we run over to Pensacola and look at some of those markers? It's been reported that Florida and Southern Georgia, north of Pensacola, have some of those stone constructions."

Carolyn thought for about half a nanosecond and said, "How's about we just relax on the front porch, drink mint juleps, and make love?"

Carolyn's remark startled Christopher at first, but he quickly replied, "Okay, but can we eat breakfast first?"

The morning passed quickly, and Carolyn and Christopher

slowly ate a lunch of finger sandwiches, salad, and iced tea on the patio of their large isolated backyard. The yard had several flower gardens and was surrounded by a neatly trimmed high oleander hedge overlooked by southern oak trees with Spanish moss. There was a gazebo with wind chimes to catch the evening sea breeze nestled between two flower gardens.

After lunch, Carolyn and Christopher decided to go over to the Fairhope Docks Marina and Yacht Club to have a safety check on their 50-foot Hinckley sailing sloop, *The Columbine*. They needed to check it out and prepare it for the summer. It took about two hours to have the boat checked and safety certified for sailing.

Later in the afternoon, Christopher was half sitting and half lying on the chaise lounge chair that was perched underneath one of the slowly moving fans hanging from the ceiling of the wide porch of Cliff House. He was gazing at the sailboats lazily crisscrossing Mobile Bay and thinking about what this bay must have looked like to the Viking explorers as they mapped the sea routes in the Gulf and explored the various inlets and bays along the Gulf Coast and Mexico.

He knew that the Zeno Narratives and legends of the Templars and Prince Madoc had hinted of the early desires of the Vikings to explore and colonize what they called Vinland, which was Canada and the United States east of the Mississippi. He had even heard stories that the explorations of Lewis and Clark had noted about the Indian legends of a white tribe of men who called themselves "Welch" who had built a fortress and towers on the island in the middle of the Ohio River below the Ohio Falls close to modern day Louisville.

President Thomas Jefferson had also heard the legends of the white tribe and tasked the Lewis and Clark expedition to investigate these legends, which is why the expedition had begun at the location in Indiana known as Clarksville. Indeed, they had seen the tall skeletons in the field east of Clarksville and the brass breastplate with Welch markings, as well as the foundations and ruins of the Templar fort built on the island. Unfortunately, when Louisville, Clarksville, and Cincinnati were built, and later farm buildings were constructed, the settlers carried away the chiseled stones to construct their buildings.

Lewis and Clark found rüne stone markers where the Missouri River joined the Mississippi River and later discovered that the Mandan Indian language was replete with words in the Welch language. Since Sacajawea, their Mandan Indian guide, could speak several Indian languages and even speak with a Welch painter accompanying the expedition, they came to the conclusion that there was some validity to the Indian legends. They later reported it to Jefferson who noted it in his diary.

Christopher was ruminating over these facts when Carolyn came to the door with two mint juleps and, after placing his on the side table next to his chair, leaned over and gently kissed his ear and whispered, "Darling, Allen is on the phone and wants to speak with you."

Christopher looked up and whispered back, "Allen?"

"Yes, you know the doctor with the beautiful daughter we met at Randall's ranch."

"Oh yes, I'm sorry. I was just sitting here dreaming about you."

"Yeah, I bet you were. With that expression on your face, I'll bet you were thinking about that Templar treasure! Anyway, Allen wants to speak to you."

"Okay," he said as he sipped his mint julep and put it back on the table next to Carolyn's mint julep. Carolyn sat down in her chair and waved at Christopher as he disappeared through the door on the way to the telephone.

Christopher picked up the telephone and said, "Hi, Allen, how are you?"

Without waiting for a reply, he continued, "What's up?"

"I just got a telephone call from Dr. John Zachary Bartholomew, an anthropologist from the University of Florida in Gainesville. You know, the one that discovered the Indian spear point in the thigh bone of an ancient giant sloth that lived in the Everglades thousands of years before scientists thought humans inhabited the area. That discovery pushed back the date of humans in North America before the Ice Age!"

"Yeah, I remember reading about that. It made quite a splash in the newspapers and startled the established scientific community—some to the point that a few die-hards still stick to their statements of it being a hoax."

"Well, you know how many individuals in the established scientific community—Allen hissed the word scientific—are all stuck-in-the-mud scientists who never had an original thought in their heads and refuse to accept anything they didn't discover themselves as a falsehood. You know the type—group thinkers! The ones who couldn't accept the fact that an amateur archeologist, Heinrich Schliemann, a businessman from Germany in 1870, had actually discovered Troy. When the scientists from the universities asked how he had the inspiration to search where he did, he told them that he just reversed the voyage of Ulysses in the legend of the Odyssey. An example of common sense over regimented scientific groupthink!"

Christopher, who had been patiently listening, shook his head and sighed into the phone, "How true. How true!"

Allen continued, "John Zachary told me he had found another unusual thing in the Everglades north of Miami—a Viking rüne stone marker—and this one mentions Lief Erikson! How about that! That means the early Vikings had probably sailed into the Gulf of Mexico. That means the Templar knights like Prince Henry Sinclair and Prince Madoc were using Viking sailing charts to create a new home base and country they called New Jerusalem on the foundations of the Enlightenment sweeping medieval Europe."

There was silence. Then Christopher choked as he said, "Wow, we are on the right track. The Templars' La Rochelle fleet split to reinforce Scottish Prince Henry's Nordic Templar settlements of New Jerusalem in Nova Scotia and New England and the southern Templar settlements of Prince Madoc in Alabama.

They were just extending the settlements originally started in Iceland, Greenland, and Nova Scotia further south. We know there were rüne stone markers in not only northern Florida, Georgia, Alabama, Mississippi, Louisiana, and the Midwest, but now, John Zachary has found a rüne stone at the southern tip of Florida that goes back to the Vikings of Leif Erikson's day."

"We also know that the Rus Vikings settled the area we now call Russia or Rus Land, as it was once known, and that the Viking Rollo settled Normandy—the land of the North men—Normans who conquered England and settled in the Orkney Islands of Scotland, and now it seems the New World!"

Allen continued, "Do you think we should go see Dr. Bartholomew and check out the rüne stone before word leaks out and something happens to it? You know how some people have an agenda and don't mind altering facts to suit them. Adolf Hitler and Napoleon were of that ilk!"

Christopher pondered what Allen had just said and said, "Yes, I think so, hang on, let me clear it with the boss."

Christopher then walked over to the porch door and said, "Allen needs to visit with us for a few days and we need to talk with a professor from the University of Florida in Gainesville. Is that okay?"

Carolyn replied, "Yes, ask him to bring Lauren—she would enjoy Fairhope—and then come back and finish your mint julep." And then she paused and smiled, "I'm not through with you yet."

Christopher returned to the phone and said, "Yes, that would be okay. Carolyn wanted me to ask you if you could bring your daughter, Lauren, with you. She would enjoy her company." And then he laughed.

"I don't think we could keep Lauren away. She is really wrapped up in this mystery. When do you want us to come?"

"Whenever you say."

"Okay, I'll check with Lauren and John Zachary and let you know."

"I'll tell you what," replied Christopher. "Call John Zachary and have him come over and bring pictures of the rüne stone. We have plenty of room and Lauren would enjoy sailing in the bay—we all would. I have a nice 50-foot sloop, *Columbine*, down at the Fairhope Docks Marina and Yacht Club, and we can spend a week talking about our plans. Call Randall and have him come too. What about Natalie and Dietrich? Have they received their leave of absence yet? Kira Ann could stay with Mary K. if she wants to, or if she wants to come here, we have plenty of room for everybody. We'll just plan on everybody visiting for a week. Okay?"

"Okay, that's a deal," said Allen, and then they hung up.

Christopher returned to the porch and his chair. He leaned over and kissed Carolyn and said, "Well, it's all set. Allen, Lauren, John Zachary Bartholomew, and his wife—if he has one—will be visiting with us next week for the week. Allen is going to check with Natalie and Dietrich and see if they have gotten their leave of absence yet. What do you think of having a bunch of guests for a week next week?"

Carolyn looked up at him and said, "Okay, sit down, just as long as I have only you for the rest of this week!"

The sun was setting and the lights of Mobile far across the bay were coming on, but the dark sky was dropping like a curtain and enveloping Cliff House and its porch, leaving Carolyn and Christopher wrapped in darkness. Carolyn rose from her chair and walked over to Christopher's chair.

Christopher had been watching the sunset fade out, and from the corner of his eye he saw Carolyn slip out of her clothes and then sit down on his lap.

He sat there stunned as she started to unbutton his shirt. He stammered, "What about any neighbors?"

She put her finger on his lips and softly said, "No one can see us," and then kissed him on his lips as he started to open his mouth to say something.

A muffled sound came from Christopher's throat and then silence as she unbuttoned his shirt slowly and rubbed his chest and then slowly unbuttoned and removed his short pants and underwear. As she put her arms around his neck and hugged and kissed him again for several minutes, she softly said, "Now isn't that better?"

10 THE GANG'S ALL HERE, ALMOST!

John Zachary Bartholomew had called and said that his white Dodge Durango SUV was acting up and he wouldn't get to Fairhope until the next day. He profusely apologized and said he would get there midmorning the next day.

Natalie, Dietrich and Kira Ann had arrived first. They had flown from Alamogordo to New Orleans and then driven the Gulf Coast route to Mobile and then Fairhope. They had stopped along the way to see the Jefferson Davis House, Beauvoir, at 2244 Beach Boulevard in Biloxi, Mississippi, that looked out over the Gulf not far from Mobile Bay.

Kira Ann was very impressed and declared, "It's beautiful and it's so close to the water."

The white sandy beach was just made for little girl's toes and she wanted to wade in the warm waters of the Gulf.

When they arrived at Cliff House, Kira Ann noticed that the house was on top of a cliff with the front lawn running down to the edge which had a neatly trimmed hedge as a fence to keep anyone from falling off. To the side was a public park with a circular drive that had a driveway descending a slight hill and then reemerging into a parking area for several vehicles. The parking area and front lawn were separated from the park by shrubbery and a low fence. From the parking area and front lawn and up a slight hill was the two-and-a-half-story Cliff House with its large porch running across the entire front- and part-side of the imposing house with its multiple car garage set into the hill under the front porch and house. Behind the garage and underground was the basement which had several rooms. The guest rooms were on the second floor, as was the master and honored guest bedroom, or in antebellum days, it would have been the grandparent's bedroom, all complete with their own baths.

Carolyn had arranged for Natalie, Dietrich and Kira Ann to have the honored guest bedroom. These two very large bedrooms looked out onto the porch and had French double doors leading to the porch. In between these bedrooms was the living room with fireplace and the dining room also with French doors opening to the porch. The four large bedrooms with bath and a smaller bedroom with bath were on the second floor. Behind the dining room and living room was a kitchen with an adjoining breakfast room, and a library with an adjoining office replete with an old-fashioned roll top desk and secretary where Christopher did his business correspondence and writing. In the corner, he had another flat-topped desk with his large Apple iMac computer with printer. Off to the side of his printer was a small reproduction statuette of Rodin's "The Thinker." Behind the office in the back was another large bedroom and bath with wide French doors that opened onto the backyard patio. The room had a door that led to a hallway connecting to the breakfast room and living room.

The stairway to the upstairs rooms was entered from the right side of the wide front porch and entered through a double French door leading into a small foyer which had an inside door leading to a hall connected to the breakfast room. Beneath the stairs and to the side of the hallway were the laundry and maintenance rooms.

Carolyn had made sure that Kira Ann had her smaller bed off to the side of the large bedroom of her parent's bedroom with a privacy screen placed between the two beds.

When Kira Ann saw the sleeping arrangements Carolyn had made, she asked her mother why she didn't have her own bedroom. Natalie smiled and picked her up and gave her a kiss on her cheek and said, "You know, sometimes here on the Gulf coast they have storms with lightning and thunder at night and Auntie Carolyn wanted to make sure that if that happened it would be easier for you to crawl into your daddy's and my bed, so you and I can curl up together, so I won't be scared."

Kira Ann thought for a minute and then said, "That was nice of her to think of us. Don't worry, Mommy, I'll protect you!" Then she threw her arms around her mother's neck and kissed her.

About that time Dietrich entered the room and Kira Ann looked up and saw him and said, "Don't worry, Daddy, I'll protect you too!"

Then she slid down out of her mother's arms and ran through the double doors to the porch, so she could see the ocean.

Dietrich stood there with a puzzled look on his face and muttered, "What was that all about?"

Natalie replied, "Think nothing of it. It was just girl talk, you wouldn't understand."

Then Natalie walked over to her husband put her arms around his neck and kissed him and said, "Let's join Kira Ann on the porch and look at the ocean." Then she added, "Won't this be fun, getting away for a week in such a romantic place? It will be just like a second honeymoon!"

Dietrich winced and quietly spoke under his breath, "Not quite!"

Later in the day, Randall, Lauren and Allen arrived. They had met in Houston and flew together on Southwest Airlines to New Orleans and rented a car to drive to Fairhope. They had stopped in Fairhope for a snack at Big Daddy's Grill for some of their famous seafood and shrimp, and then spent some time looking at downtown Fairhope before going on to Cliff House.

When they arrived at the driveway to Cliff House, Lauren exclaimed, "Boy, am I going to like this. Just look at that beach with its white sand and that fabulous bay. It's perfect for sailing. Look across the bay, I can almost see Mobile. This is fantastic. I'll bet we will be able to see the stars tonight."

Allen chimed in and told her, "Yes, and I believe that Carolyn and Christopher have a sailing boat. Maybe they'll let you sail it."

Lauren looked at her father and said, "Gee pops, I hope it's not a Sunfish."

Allen replied, "I think it's bigger than that. We'll see."

Randall, who was driving the rental car smiled as he turned into the driveway and said, "I think you'll like it. Well here we are. Cliff House!"

They drove to the parking place in front of the house and got out of the car. Lauren got out first and walked over to the hedge on the cliff looked down the beach at the coconut palm trees and turned around to her father and exclaimed, "Look at those coconut palms, just like Hawaii."

Allen walked to her side and put his arm around her shoulder and said, "Does my number one daughter like it?"

She looked up at him and replied, "What do you mean number one? I'm your only daughter," and then she gave Allen an impish grin and poked him in his side with a finger and said, "Aren't I?"

He laughed and just at that moment, Natalie, Dietrich, Kira Ann, Carolyn and Christopher arrived to greet them and help with the luggage.

Kira Ann broke loose from her mother's grip and ran to Lauren and put her arms around Lauren's waist and hugged her tight. She looked up at Lauren and said, "I'm so glad you're here and so is mommy and daddy."

Lauren reached down and stroked Kira's long hair and muttered, "Me too."

They all walked back to the house and were taken to their rooms. Lauren was placed in the large rear bedroom overlooking the patio and rear flower gardens while Allen and

Randall occupied two of the four bedrooms upstairs.

After everyone was refreshed, they joined Carolyn, Natalie, Kira Ann, Christopher and Dietrich on the wide front porch with several fans hanging from its ceiling. The fans were slowly moving to keep any flying insects away even though the mosquitoes were not out in force yet.

Kira Ann was examining the various multicolored flowers in their pots lining the wide outside edge of the porch that extended beyond the its polished cedar railing while her father was engaged in a conversation with Christopher about Prince Madoc's colony in Fairhope so long ago.

Carolyn and Natalie were checking out the grill that Christopher had placed on the porch where he was going to fix shish kabob with baked potato and salad with all of the dressings and a side dish of fresh fruit and Southern pecan pie with ice cream as a dessert. Kira Ann seemed to be more interested in the dessert than the main course, maybe because she knew Lauren liked ice cream and could help her get an extra portion of her favorite—Neapolitan!

Christopher and Dietrich had placed two large round tables and chairs for the eight adventurers. She and Christopher had also arranged for two maids to help with the serving and cleanup, so their guests could spend more time together on their first night.

They were all disappointed that John Zachary would not be there for their first night, and Allen explained that his professor friend at the University of Florida was a very interesting archeologist and anthropologist all wrapped up in his work. He explained that he was kind of an Indiana Jones person who looked more like Teddy Roosevelt than Harrison Ford and that he was not married because of his research schedule and fieldwork although he had a girlfriend he adored who was trying to slow him down enough to get him to the altar.

Kira Ann asked Allen, "Who was Teddy Roosevelt?"

Everyone smiled waiting for Allen's response.

"He was a president of the United States that had a big statue of him carved on the side of a mountain."

"Oh, you mean Mount Rushmore in the Black Hills in South Dakota? Was he the one with the glasses?"

Everyone laughed, and even Allen had to smile. He looked over to Lauren and she was smiling and said, "Well, pops!"

Allen responded, "Yes, he wore glasses, and …."

Before he could complete his sentence, Kira Ann interrupted and asked, "Was he the president that was named after the teddy bear?"

By this time everyone was chuckling, and Lauren felt obliged to help her father out of his predicament.

She went over to Kira Ann and picked her up, squeezed her, and said softly, "No, it is the other way around. They named the teddy bear after him."

"Oh, I see. Is John Zachary soft and cuddly?"

By this time even Lauren was speechless and holding back her laughter.

"Darling, I guess we'll just have to wait and see tomorrow."

Allen had his hand over his mouth and stifled his laughter.

About that time a maid named Sue announced that dinner was ready. The maids had already fixed the shish kabob and had everything laid out on the tables for them. Carolyn had made tea for them and milk for Kira Ann.

Meanwhile Kira Ann managed to sit next to Lauren.

That night was absolutely beautiful. The bay water was still and the Lyrid meteor shower over Mobile Bay was spectacular.

Everyone went to bed happy wanting to meet John Zachary the next day and see if he was soft and cuddly.

11 THE PLAN

Everyone had finished breakfast and were sitting on the front porch of Cliff House waiting for John Zachary Bartholomew to arrive. That is everyone except Kira Ann and Lauren who were walking barefoot in the soft white sand of the beach. They were walking toward the Ecor Rouge cliffs when two white pelicans swooped down and scooped up two fish that had come too close to the surface of the water. The pelicans resembled two dive bombers attacking an enemy. Kira Ann was surprised at the suddenness of the apparently aimless flight of the birds turning suddenly into a vicious attack.

Lauren turned to Kira Ann and explained that in nature caution and awareness of surroundings and possible danger could come from any quarter and that humans, like animals, must be alert and aware of the possibilities of danger at all times and take necessary precautions. She further mentioned that when we go sailing we must be aware of all weather conditions and be able to chart a course that would be safe from all possible harm.

Kira Ann listened intently and then said, "Is that why mommy always says that I should always think ahead of all of the possible consequences of anything I say or do?"

"Yes, your mother is wise to tell you that."

"Daddy always tells me to just don't go where trouble might be."

Lauren smiled and said, "My daddy always used to say Confucius says storm is easier to find than still water."

Kira Ann thought for a minute, turned her face up, and looked into Lauren's eyes and asked, "Who is Confucius?"

"Confucius was a very wise man who lived 2,500 years ago in China. My father once gave me a book about him and his sayings about life. He was a philosopher and counselor to the emperor of China."

"Do you think my daddy would give me a book about Confucius?"

Lauren replied, "I'm sure he would, but I would be happy to give you my book, or if you want we can go to the Page and Palette bookstore here in Fairhope. I saw it when my father, Dr. Fox, and I had lunch downtown yesterday when we arrived."

Kira Ann's face brightened, and she said, "Okay, I would like to read it. My mother and father always buy me such interesting books."

Lauren stopped walking, and Kira Ann went over to her and grabbed her hand. This was the first time she had heard Kira Ann refer to her parents as mother and father rather than mommy and daddy. She thought to herself, "Wow, she's more grown up than I thought!"

Lauren looked down and said, "Why don't we head back to the house? Dr. Fox's friend, Dr. John Zachary Bartholomew, should be arriving soon."

They turned, and Kira Ann asked, "Do you think Dr. Bartholomew would mind if I called him, Dr. John?"

"I don't know, let's ask him when he arrives."

"Okay," Kira Ann said in a soft voice.

They walked hand-in-hand back to Cliff House. It took them about twenty minutes, and they arrived tired but refreshed by the sea breeze. The sun was getting higher in the sky and the sand was starting to get warm.

Kira Ann remarked, "If we walk on the sand later, we should probably put our shoes on, don't you think?"

Lauren said, "You're correct. Confucius say, 'It is better to carry shoes with you when you walk on beach.'"

Kira Ann looked up at Lauren with a quizzical expression, "He didn't really say that, did he?"

Lauren replied, "No, but he should have!"

Lauren squeezed Kira Ann's hand gently and they both laughed at their joke.

Natalie was standing at the top of the stairway down to the beach, and when the two strollers reached the top of the stairs, Natalie said, "Both of you probably should have taken your shoes. I imagine the sand is getting fairly warm by now!"

The two strollers looked at each other and laughed.

Natalie looked at them both with a confused look on her face and said, "What's so funny?"

Lauren looked down at Kira Ann and then up to Natalie and said, "Nothing really. I just promised Kira Ann that I would buy her a book about Confucius and his quotations at the Pages and Palettes bookstore downtown."

"Oh, now I see. Confucius sometimes also says, 'sometimes mothers put foot in own mouth.'"

Kira looked at her mother and remarked, "Oh, you've read Confucius' book too?"

All three of them started laughing and were still grinning when they walked up the stairs to the porch at Cliff House. There, Dietrich saw his wife and daughter and Lauren with big grins on their faces.

Dietrich grinned and said, "What's so funny?"

Kira Ann replied, "Oh Daddy, it's a girl thing!"

Natalie and Lauren bent over howling with laughter.

Dietrich shook his head and walked into the house with Lauren, his wife, and daughter, and Carolyn looked at them and asked, "What's up?"

Dietrich replied, "Don't ask. It's a girl thing!"

It was about an hour later that a white Dodge Durango SUV

with four-wheel drive pulled in to the parking spaces in front of Cliff House.

Everyone was standing on the porch watching as a five-foot-eight-inch tall man with a medium athletic build and wavy dark hair, and sporting a Teddy Roosevelt bushy mustache, stepped out of the truck. He was wearing a khaki rolled-up sleeve hunting shirt with epaulets, khaki pants, and holding his brown Indiana Jones fedora hat in one hand and a leather-bound journal in the other. He had wire rimmed sunglasses that had slid half way down his nose. His face and arms were tanned, and the tip of his nose was sunburned.

Dr. Bartholomew looked up and saw everyone looking at him and waved his left hand with a slight flipping motion and shouted, "Hi, y'all."

Kira Ann was holding her father's hand and pulled him down so she could whisper into his ear, "He does look like Teddy Roosevelt!"

Dietrich murmured, "Yes, he does, but he sounds Southern."

Kira Ann let go of her father's hand and caught up with Carolyn and Christopher who were walking down the stairs to the driveway. She passed them and ran ahead and reached her hand out to shake Dr. Bartholomew's leathery hand. He smiled and picked her up, and Kira Ann grinned and said, "Dr. Bartholomew …."

And before she could finish her sentence, he said, "Just call me Zach."

"Okay, Dr. Zach, I'm Kira Ann." She turned in his arms and pointed to her parents and announced, "That's my mother and father on the porch."

Dr. Zach waved at them with his left hand holding his hat and shouted, "Pleased to meet you!" And then he let Kira Ann down to the driveway, transferred his leather journal to the hand holding his hat, and shook Carolyn and Christopher's hands, saying, "Sure happy to meet both of you and thank you very much for asking me to visit with everyone."

Kira Ann ran back to her parents, and as she passed Lauren,

she whispered to her, "He wants to be called Zach."

Lauren and Allen smiled and nodded their heads.

Christopher grabbed Zach's luggage and led him up the stairway, so he could meet everyone. He motioned for everyone to grab a chair after greeting Zach while he took Zach's luggage upstairs to his room.

When he returned to the porch, everyone was sitting around the four tables on the porch and talking. Carolyn had the two maids serve some cold lemonade to go with the assorted nuts and fresh fruits in a variety of bowls with serving plates and silverware. Some finger sandwiches, deviled eggs, potato chips, and onion dip were on the extra fourth table in a buffet fashion.

Zach had washed his hands when he was pushed into the kitchen to help carry some of the luncheon items to the tables on the porch. Carolyn had told him that it was every man for himself and everyone was expected to clean up after themselves. She had laid out the rules of the house to everyone in a similar fashion.

By the time everyone had met Zach and shared a meal with him, they felt they had known him for a long time. He was genial, good natured, and willing to share his knowledge with them. Kira Ann said she would rather go to Aunt Carolyn's and Uncle Christopher's library and read a book she had previously found there.

The sun was starting to retreat when Randall asked Zach to tell them a little of his anthropological digs around the Moore Haven area of the southeast corner of Lake Okeechobee in South Florida. He told them about his find of a spearhead in the thighbone of a giant ancient sloth, and his recent find of a rüne stone with Nordic writing that mentioned Leif Erikson and had the same hooked X seen in other American rüne stones. He also explained how this establishes the fact that the early Vikings had made it to the Caribbean around Key West and up the Gulf Coast to the mouth of the Mississippi River and perhaps to Mexico and the Aztecs who described white men with beards and big canoes or ships with wings (sails).

He continued, by illustrating how the early Viking explorations set up the later plans of Queen Margarette and the Templars to establish a new colony to the west called New Jerusalem. He explained that the Templars put all of their treasure and records on eighteen ships when they sailed to France from their fortress home on Crete.

Both the Hospitallers and the Templars were planning on opening new headquarters elsewhere on other islands rather than their crowded situation with two rival Orders on the same island. The Hospitallers were planning to conquer the island of Rhodes, which they later did. Although invited, the Hospitallers did not sail to France to meet the pope as the Templars did, and fortunately did not meet the same fate as the Templars who were planning to move from Crete to New Jerusalem. They were only making a temporary stop in France to meet the pope and recover their treasure from their temple in Paris.

Zach further postulated that is why they took their whole fleet to the port of La Rochelle on the western side of France. The Templars transported part of their treasure and records from the Paris temple in wagons to their banking headquarters in Geneva and Bern. The other part of their treasure and records in Paris they transported in wagons to the eighteen ships waiting in La Rochelle to add to their treasure and records from Crete.

They intended to split the treasure on the ships with the bulk of it in the twelve ships going to Scotland for safekeeping until they could transfer it to the northern part of New Jerusalem in the Nova Scotia-New England area. The remaining six ships and their smaller treasure was intended to go to the southern part of New Jerusalem where the Templar Prince Madoc had earlier established a settlement of Irish and Welsh settlers at the headwaters of Mobile Bay in what is now Fairhope, Alabama.

Zach continued to say that the puzzle was why the leadership and the grand master of the Knights Templar, Jacques de Molay, loaded their treasure and records from Crete onto those eighteen ships if they were going back to Crete after dropping off their leaders and grand master to meet with Pope Clement V and King Philip IV in Marseille?

Why did the fleet of eighteen ships sail through the Straits of Gibraltar into the Bay of Biscay and then anchor at La Rochelle unless they were planning to sail north? Why not just stay at anchor in Marseilles before sailing back to Crete? And why would they load up all of their wealth and goods in the first place just to visit the king of France and the pope in Marseille and then have to tote them all the way back to Crete?

The answer is, they were cleaning house and moving somewhere else!

King Phillip IV was called "the fair" for his good looks, not his character which was described by the Bishop of Pamiers, Bernard Saisset, as neither man nor beast, but rather a cold statue. It was King Philip IV with the complicity of Pope Clement V that had the Knights Templar, its leaders, grand master, and some of the other Knights Templar in France arrested on Friday the 13th of October 1307, jailed, tortured, and later burned at the stake.

Zach postulated that the reason nobody found any treasure or records on Crete after the Inquisition and dissolution of the Knights Templar was because the Knights Templar were actually moving from Crete to their new home in New Jerusalem!

He continued to say that the grand master and some of the Templar leaders planned to go in twelve ships with the bulk of their records and treasure to Scotland because they knew they had protection and safe haven there with the king of Scotland, Robert the Bruce, and the Saint Clair and Seton Templar families. From Scotland they were planning to move their new headquarters safely to the Nova Scotia-New England area somewhere around the Saint Lawrence Seaway.

The other leaders and Knights Templar were going to sail the other six ships to Fairhope with a minor portion of their treasure to consolidate their position in the southern part of their new colony of New Jerusalem which had been earlier settled by Prince Madoc and his Irish and Welsh settlers that sailed from Ireland in 1170 as a vanguard for his later voyages and settler migrations to Fairhope.

They all agreed with his theory about all of these various findings and expressed disbelief that nobody had connected all of the dots.

Zach replied, "And that a lack of connecting all the history of exploration along with politics, the untimely death of Queen Margarette was partly responsible. Although, in Queen Elizabeth's Court, her followers had argued that England owned all of North America since the voyages of Prince Madoc to the New World in 1170 and to North America with his Welsh and Irish settlers."

Queen Elizabeth the First's Court also pointed out that Prince Henry Sinclair of Scotland had sailed to North America in 1396 as well as John Cabot's voyage to North America in 1407 and the fact that Sir Francis Drake had circumnavigated the globe in his single voyage from 1577 to 1578 and set foot in Puerto Rico and Jamaica, Panama, and the West coast of California as proof of English claims there. Queen Elizabeth I of England used all of these facts so she could lay claim to all of North America from the Gulf of Mexico to Hudson's Bay.

The day had quietly slipped into night, and after Zach's explanation of New Jerusalem, they felt they should stop and rest awhile before dinner. They left the porch and retired to their rooms.

Kira Ann had wandered back to the porch as Zach concluded his lecture. She went up to Natalie and said, "Mommy, I'm hungry, when do you think we'll have dinner? It's already 5:30."

Natalie put her finger to her lips and whispered, "Pretty soon. Everyone will probably want to go to their rooms and freshen up a bit before dinner."

"Did Aunty Carolyn mention what we are going to have for dessert? I know that Uncle Christopher and Miss Lauren will want some ice cream."

Kira Ann looked at her mother and with a slight smile, she

figured she had made a good case for her favorite dessert.

"I don't know," Natalie replied. "But I'll ask her and let you know. Why don't you sit here on the porch and watch the boats and the sunset?"

"Okay," Kira Ann replied and then walked over to an empty chaise lounge and sat down.

She turned her head to her mother and said, "Is it okay if I take a small nap?"

"Yes," Natalie replied and then walked into the kitchen to talk with Carolyn who was instructing the two maids about the evening meal and where to serve it.

A few clouds were starting to drift over the bay and quietly were joined by some dark angry looking clouds that were building into thunderclouds. In an hour there were a few lightning flashes, and a distant rumble of thunder was starting to roll across the bay and the wind was picking up. A few drops of rain dropped onto the flower pots and flowers lining the porch.

Kira Ann's chaise lounge chair was turned toward the bay so that a few of the rain drops were blown past the porch railing and onto Kira Ann's feet. She had placed her shoes aside on the porch next to her chair and a few drops of rain had dropped on her toes and aroused her from her nap. She woke up, rubbed her eyes, and saw the distant flash of lightning followed by the deep rumble of thunder.

Her eyes widened, and she saw the waves on the beach rising with a few whitecaps starting to appear. She quickly leaned down, picked up her socks and shoes and ran through the door to the living room and then into the kitchen. The two maids were nonchalantly absorbed in fixing the evening meal and had not even noticed the storm outside starting to build. Kira told them that it was starting to rain and there was lightning and wind. They calmly looked at her and explained that evening storms were common in the spring and not to worry.

Even though the waves were getting high, Cliff House was atop a thirty-foot cliff protected from the waves below.

Kira Ann marveled at their calm demeanor and she was determined that she would be as brave and calm as they were. She left the kitchen and went to her and her parent's bedroom where her father was calmly reading the local newspaper, *The Fairhope Courier*, which has been published since 1894. Her mother was in the bathroom taking a shower.

Kira walked over to Dietrich and said calmly, "Daddy, I'm a big girl and I am not afraid of the bad storm outside."

Just as she said that, there was the crackle of lightning outside close to the house and the instant crash of thunder. Her eyes widened, and she leaped into Dietrich's lap and put her arms around his neck.

Dietrich looked down at his daughter and put his arms around her and cradled her, gently rocking back and forth and softly said, "That was close, don't you think?"

She looked up and calmly said, "Yes, awfully close." And then she laid her head against her father's chest as he gently rocked her back and forth.

12 THE JIGSAW PUZZLE

The next day the morning sky was clear with no evidence of the fearful thunderstorm that had raged the night before except for some leaves from the trees strewn on the trimmed grass lawn and a few broken flowers in the flower beds of Cliff House. There were a few palm branches on the beach, but no other apparent damage.

The breakfast room was alive with the chatter of conversation between the adventurers sitting around the breakfast table. Kira Ann was sitting next to John Zachary and asking him about the rather beat up brown fedora hat he was holding in his hand the day before. He told her it was the hat he wore while exploring in the Everglades and that sometimes he pinned the left side of the brim to the crown of the hat as the Australians often did when he was in thick brush.

Kira Ann accepted the remark without any questions because it seemed logical to her.

Seated on the other side of John Zachary was Lauren and next to her, her father, Allen. Lauren said that she thought his lecture the day before was very interesting and added a dimension to American history that she didn't know. He had told her that history was often distorted by historians that had an agenda or politicians who usually distort history to fit their usual position, which invariably was based on money, power and ego.

Lauren and Allen nodded their heads in agreement and Lauren commented, "It all seems like a disparate assortment of facts that seems not to be connected."

"Oh, you mean like a jigsaw puzzle?"

Kira Ann looked up to John Zachary and said, "I'm good with jigsaw puzzles. I can usually recognize the shapes and fit the pieces together."

"You mean shapes, colors and images don't you?" replied Zach.

"Yes, that's what I mean. I fit the pieces together because it looks correct."

Lauren was listening intently and then interjected, "You mean common sense, don't you?"

John Zachary rubbed his forehead and admitted, "Yes, that's exactly what she means."

Allen upon hearing that, smiled at Kira Ann and Lauren and whispered, "You mean, Confucius says…."

Kira Ann and Lauren looked at each other and immediately laughed.

"Ah, pops, there you go again," sighed Lauren.

Zach, who had been listening to this interplay, remarked, "I think I understand. Common sense has been around for a long time, hasn't it?"

Lauren looked at John Zachary and said, "But usually not appreciated, huh?"

Zach looked around the table at everyone, covered his mouth, and then cleared his throat. Everyone looked at him, and he said, "I've just been talking with my fellow philosophers, Kira Ann, Lauren and Allen, and want to ask you all if you would like to play a game this morning? The game is to fit the pieces of a jigsaw puzzle together!"

They all looked at each other, and everyone agreed that would be interesting. Even Kira Ann raised her hand and proclaimed that she would like to play the game.

Natalie turned to her precocious daughter and then Dietrich and said, "Maybe for a little while, but I think your Uncle Christopher has a new jigsaw puzzle in his study."

She looked at Christopher as she said the word study.

He immediately caught the drift of her remark and said to Kira Ann, "If you get tired of Zach's virtual reality jigsaw puzzle, I think you will like the new puzzle I got just for you when I heard you would be visiting with your Aunt Carolyn and me. Okay?"

Kira Ann looked at her cousin and said, "Okay, I think I understand. He's going to describe the jigsaw pieces, and we have to visualize them and then put them together in our minds."

Christopher nodded his head in the affirmative.

"Okay, I'll try it for a while."

Allen was smiling and leaned over to his daughter and whispered, "She is just like you when you were her age."

Lauren whispered back, "Yeah."

Carolyn then stood up, and as she motioned to the two maids to help clean up the dishes, she said, "Okay, Would you all like to retire to the front porch or the front room for the discussion?"

Randall piped up and said, "How about the living room and the comfortable sofas and chairs?" Then he added, "Besides it's closer to the kitchen and the bathrooms."

Everyone smiled and withdrew to the living room to allow the maids to do their jobs.

After everyone was comfortably seated, Zach stood in front of them and started to speak.

"Let us all pretend that we are all eagles flying above the forest high enough to see all of the bits of information that I will describe. We don't want to be like the woodpeckers below on the bark of the facts in the forest searching for grubs or prejudice."

Everyone immediately grasped what he was saying, including Kira Ann who raised her hand and said, "I don't want to be a woodpecker making a lot of noise. I would rather be an eagle flying high in the sky, so I can see the jigsaw pieces!"

Lauren turned to Kira Ann who was sitting next to her and smiled and then to her father on her other side and whispered into his ear, "Out of the mouth of babes!" She then turned back to Kira Ann and whispered into her ear, "Me too!"

Zach continued after the ripple of chuckling subsided, "Yes, let's look at the facts. Can anyone tell me what the flag of Nova Scotia and the flag of Scotland look like?"

Randall immediately raised his hand and said, "Yes, they are the same except the Nova Scotia flag has the shield and rampant red lion emblem of Scotland at the crossing of the white saltire cross bars on the blue background. The flag of Saint Andrew and the ancient flag of Saint Patrick of Ireland was a red saltire cross on a white background.

"Where was Prince Henry of Orkney from?" Zach asked, and then he answered, "From Scotland."

"What is the flag of the Mi'qmaq Indians?" Zach again asked and then answered, "A white flag with a red cross with a red half-moon in one upper corner and a red star in the other upper corner. It's the Templar flag and the flag of England without the star and half-moon, which are Indian mystic symbols. Remember, Richard the Lion Hearted of England was a Templar! The Union Jack used by the UK today is an overlay of the English, Scottish, and Irish flags. The duke of Wales is the title of the heir apparent to the British Crown. So, the flag of England is the Knights Templar flag, same as the Mi'qmaq Indians.

"What is the flag of Switzerland?" and then Zach continued the game of answering his own questions, "The flag of the Order of Saint John, which the Knights Templar joined after the Inquisition of 1307. A red flag with a white cross.

"What is the flag of Malta? It's the flag of the Order of Saint John. A red flag with a white cross.

"What was the flag of the Virgin Islands of Saint John, Saint Croix, Saint Thomas, Saint Martin, Saint Barthélemy, and Saint Christopher that the Hospitaller Order of Saint John ruled from 1651 to 1665? The flag of the Hospitaller Order of Saint

John where the Knights Templar were hiding out. The United States bought the Virgin Islands of Saint Croix, Saint John, and Saint Thomas in 1916 from the kingdom of Denmark-Norway as naval bases to counter the German submarine threat of World War I.

"What was the flag of the kingdom of Denmark, Norway, and Sweden during the reign of Queen Margarette in 1396 when Prince Henry sailed to Nova Scotia, Vinland, and New England? You guessed it. It was the flag of the Hospitaller Order of Saint John!

"The flag of the kingdom of Denmark today is the flag of the Hospitaller Order of Saint John except the center of the white cross is pulled to the left so when the flag is placed over the coffin of the Danish Monarch, it is over the heart of the Danish monarch. It has been that way since the earliest days of the Danish Monarchy."

Zach continued by saying, "Let's take a look at the sails of the Niña, Pinta and Santa Maria. The main white linen sails of all three ships were marked with the red cross of the Knights Templar. Remember that the Knights Templar were not persecuted in Spain or Portugal. They were protected by the kings of those two countries. They were and still are known there as the Knights of Christ and an Order of the crown. The original name of the Templar Order was the Poor Fellow-Soldiers of Christ and the Temple of Solomon which people of the time just shortened to Knights Templar rather than the jaw breaking actual name."

Kira Ann turned to Lauren and whispered, "What does he mean by jaw breaking?"

Lauren whispered back, "He means long drawn out."

Kira Ann whispered back, "Why didn't he just say that?"

Lauren was surprised at her reply and whispered back, "Do you understand all of this?"

Kira Ann whispered back, "Of course, don't you?"

Lauren was stunned. A six-year-old going on twenty!

Zach continued, "The Virgin Islands were discovered by Columbus on his second voyage and named for Saint Ursula and her virgin followers."

Lauren gasped and glanced at Kira Ann. She didn't seem to be concerned about what Zach had just said.

She shrugged her shoulders and turned her attention back to Zach.

Zach continued on and was explaining that Columbus was married to Felipa Monez-Parastrelo who was Portuguese and a noblewoman whose family members were Knights Templar and supported their causes. Felipa's brother governed Porto Santo in Madeira, where the son of Elizabeth Sinclair and Sir John Drummond had met and married into the family of Columbus's in-laws. When he married Felipa, Columbus gained access to a trove of secret charts and maps. Knowledge of four hundred years of Norse ventures in the West, as well as the hundred-year-old saga of grandfather Henry Sinclair's voyages fell into Columbus' hands. Historians believe that Columbus actually had one of the Zeno maps that were made during Prince Henry Sinclair and Antonio Zeno's earlier first voyage to Nova Scotia to prepare for his later 1398 voyage. It was on that voyage with his flotilla of twelve ships carrying the Templar treasure to Nova Scotia or New England that Prince Henry Sinclair carried out Queen Margarette's dream and plan to create a New Jerusalem.

It was on Madeira that Columbus decided to cross the Atlantic. The experiences he gained sailing in the island chain of Madeira served to give him the confidence to consider his own voyage across the Atlantic. After 1479 he was ready to make the voyage, but could find no financial backers. After many years, he finally persuaded Queen Isabella and King Ferdinand of Spain to finance his voyage. They had just defeated the last of the Muslim armies and forced them out of Spain and were willing to back him for the wealth he promised them when he sailed westward to China, circumventing the Silk Road controlled by the Muslims.

It has been said that one of his captains, Martin Alonzo Pinzon from Palos, Spain, had already been to the Americas and now commanded the Pinta for Columbus. He had been the navigator for a ship owned by Jean Cousins of France that was blown far off its course by a violent storm in the Atlantic and wound up either in North or South America, or so he claimed after Columbus' voyage.

King Henry, the Navigator, of Portugal had encouraged exploration and Portugal's discoveries which encouraged Queen Isabella and King Ferdinand to take the risk.

The problem for Columbus on his voyage to the New World was that he was sailing a longer route west by way of the Canary Islands at a latitude of 28 degrees rather than the shorter northern great circle route used by the Vikings and modern airplanes and ships to reach America from Europe. He miscalculated the distance, which took longer and almost created a mutiny with his crew since they were running short of food and water. He reached the Bahamas in the nick of time!"

Kira again turned to Lauren and whispered, "What does the nick of time mean?" As soon as she said it she added, "Oh, I know, just in time. Sorry." She then turned back toward Zach and cradled her chin with the palms of her hands and continued listening.

Lauren shrugged her shoulders again and then cradled her chin with her hands as she listened to Zach.

Allen, who noticed all of this, thought to himself, "Two peas in a pod." And then he smiled.

Zach was winding down his virtual reality jigsaw puzzle by saying, "The Scottish Rite Masonic Order to which our founding fathers belonged has a higher degree attained by a few of their members which is called the Knights Templar degree. The Blue Lodge of the English is a later fraternal red herring created to mimic the older Scottish Frére Maçon within the Hospitaller Order of Saint John, which later became the Scottish Rite Masonic Order. The Blue Lodge was created as The Grand Lodge of England in London in 1717. The color blue to describe the Grand Lodge of England represents brotherhood, and they co-opted the rituals of Scottish Rite Free Masonry for their own.

"Now that we have laid out the pieces of the puzzle, we can see that there are a number of markers that point to the Knights Templar and the Order of Saint John, the Scottish Rite Free Masons and the Enlightenment, the Viking and Prince Henry Sinclair's voyages and their friendship with the Abenaki Indians, which lasts to this day in Nova Scotia Canada. All point to a secret leading to the lost treasure of the eighteen Templar ships anchored in La Rochelle Harbor on the night of Thursday the 12th and morning of Friday the 13th of October1307.

"We know about the Templar connections with Prince Madoc and his settlers in Fairhope, Alabama, and their friendship with the Creek and Cherokee Indians and their Templar connections with Prince Henry Sinclair of Orkney and his friendship with the Abenaki Indians and the desire of Queen Margarette to create a new nation in the West lands which were found earlier by Leif Erikson on his voyages. We also must include the rune stones with the hooked X markers left by the Cistercian monks from Göttland that accompanied these later explorations. So, what does all of this mean?

"All of the legends, the history, and the tangible evidence we can look at points to the Nova Scotia-New England area as the likely place where the treasure is. Just what the attempted theft of the Yale Brasher Doubloon by the Muslim Brotherhood or their attempt to kidnap the Mi'qmaq grand chief means is a mystery. Somehow, they know something we don't."

Lauren raised her hand and said, "What about the letter Ephraim Brasher wrote to George Washington when he could have just walked next door and given it to him or just told him what the contents of the letter was since they were neighbors on Cherry Street in New York? I understand that he was a close friend of Washington during the Revolutionary War. He was a lieutenant in Colonel John Lasher's regiment in New York early in the Revolutionary War."

Zach looked at her with a bewildered look and said, "I didn't know that. Are you sure?"

Lauren replied, "Right as rain, I'm pretty sure. Ever since pops, ah, I mean my father told me about Washington's Doubloon, I have been looking up the history of Ephraim Brasher and George Washington and the unique coin he made for only George Washington.

"I also found out that Ephraim Brasher knew Alexander Hamilton, President Washington's Treasury secretary, and William Saint Clair and General Arthur Saint Clair who became the first governor of the Old Northwest Territory after the Revolutionary War.

"All of them served on George Washington's staff during the Revolutionary War and were present at the Queen Charlotte, or Faunce's Inn and Tavern as they called it then in New York, when General George Washington gave his farewell address to his general staff after the end of the Revolutionary War!"

Zach, Randall, and Allen were all startled at this information.

Zach took a deep breath and slowly let it out as he said, "This is wonderful news. So all of them may have had knowledge of the secret."

Lauren replied, "I don't think so. I think it was for President Washington's eyes only!"

Randall sighed, "Then we are back where we started and still don't know what the Muslim Brotherhood is up to!"

Lauren then looked at Kira Ann and then her father and said, "Confucius and Jesus both said, 'Let them with eyes, see, and them with ears, hear!'" Then she smiled and both Kira Ann and Allen nodded their heads.

13 AN OLD NEMESIS

The red sun was rising up out of Mobile Bay looking like the head of Neptune rising from a night's sleep. Lauren had gotten up before dawn and dressed in a white tank top and shorts with slippers on her feet. She then slipped downstairs to the kitchen. She was the only one awake and tried not to make any noise that might awaken the household.

She took the pitcher of orange juice out of the refrigerator and poured herself a glass, placed her multivitamin capsule in her mouth, and washed it down with a gulp of the juice. She was up early because she wanted to take a picture of the sunrise over the bay. She was carrying her Apple iPhone in her left hand as she strolled through the living room toward the front door to the porch. She spied Christopher's sea binoculars with its high magnification zoom lenses and put its strap around her neck.

She carefully opened the door and stepped through it onto the well-polished cypress wood floor, quietly closed the door, and sought out one of the chairs lined up the length of the porch. She decided she would take a place next to a red rose vine that had climbed onto the porch railing next to a pillar. The spot was in the middle of the porch and offered a wonderful view of the bay. As she sat down and looked out toward the bay, she noticed one lonely O'Day 23 sloop anchored about 500 yards dead center to Cliff House with its main mast sticking up in the center of the rising orb of the sun

She first thought, "Oh, darn! I was hoping there wouldn't be any vessels out this early," and then it occurred to her that the boat must have been anchored there all night. Then she mused to herself, "Probably some honeymoon couple that anchored there last night to watch the sunset and decided to stay the night and catch the sunrise the next morning."

Her thoughts immediately turned to her boyfriend working himself to death back in Los Angeles. A smile crossed her face as she raised her iPhone and snapped several pictures of the sun and bay at different angles and magnifications. She even used the high resolution zoom feature of her iPhone camera to get a close-up of the boat gently swaying at anchor silhouetted dead center to the rising sun, giving her enough light to notice the couple sitting astern of the boat's cabin.

She thought to herself, "That doesn't look like a honeymoon couple. They seem to have their backs to the sun and looking this way toward the beach, and it looks like one of them is holding some binoculars!"

Disappointed that it was not the romantic couple she was hoping was there, she instinctively moved behind the pillar with the red rose vine clinging to it. Then she looked at the close up picture of the couple on the boat. It clearly showed two men of Middle Eastern descent. "That's odd," she thought.

"What would they be doing anchored there? Were they fishing? No, there weren't any fishing poles, and besides it looked like one of the men—the one with the binoculars—was looking straight at her!"

She put her iPhone down on the side table beside her chair and reached for her binoculars.

She looked for an opening in the bushes behind the porch railing where she could get a view of the boat without being seen.

She spotted one and got down on her knees and crawled to it. She then looked to see if she could see the boat.

She could!

She raised the binoculars to her eyes and when she found the boat, she slid the zoom lever of the binoculars to their full magnification. The sun had swiftly risen out of the sea to the point that she could make out the men's features and saw that the man with the binoculars was talking to the other one who was responding in an animated way—raising his right hand and arm as if to make an important point.

He was now pointing to the man and then started to shake his fist. The man with the binoculars lowered them so they hung by the leather strap around his neck and rested on his chest. He had a scowl on his face and appeared to engage in a heated discussion with the other man. Then the man without the binoculars turned and stormed into the cabin.

Lauren grabbed her iPhone and took a zoomed-in picture of the man with the scowl on his face.

About this time, Natalie and Dietrich with Kira Ann close behind them came through the front door to their bedroom onto the porch. All three were still wearing their bed clothes and Natalie and Kira Ann immediately saw Lauren down on her knees behind the oleander bush in front of the railing.

Natalie almost whispered to her, "What are you doing? Did you lose something?"

Kira Ann ran over to her and knelt down beside Lauren and asked her, "Can I help you find it? What is it you're looking for?"

Dietrich, upon hearing Natalie and seeing Kira Ann rush over to Lauren, said in a typical male fashion, "What's going on?"

Lauren grabbed Kira and pulled her down beside her and spoke to Natalie and Dietrich, "Go back inside before he sees you!"

Dietrich stepped back, grasping Natalie around her waist, and pulled the curtain from the window next to the door so as to obscure them from being seen.

Natalie had a frightened look on her face, and Dietrich wore a puzzled smile on his face. Kira Ann seemed composed, curious, and willing to help in any way she could.

Lauren spoke almost in a whisper and said, "There are two guys in a sailboat anchored about 500 yards out in the bay in front of this house and they have been apparently there for some time before sunrise watching this house with binoculars.

"I hope it's merely a coincidence, but it looks suspicious. The two guys look like they are from the Middle East and they don't look happy. I've been watching them since sunrise and I think I got a pretty good close up picture of them."

Lauren turned to Kira Ann who was sitting next to her doppelgänger friend and with an innocent smile said, "Why would they do that?"

Lauren looked back at her friend and said, "Let's crawl over to your mother and dad and go inside so we can talk about it."

As she said that, Natalie put her hand to her mouth, drew her negligee around her nightgown, and whispered to Dietrich, "New Orleans all over again!"

When Kira Ann and Lauren had crawled over and entered their bedroom, Dietrich closed the door and the four of them walked over to the bed.

Natalie said to Kira Ann, "Now that we have been thoroughly invigorated, why don't you go ahead and take your shower and get dressed for breakfast."

Kira Ann dropped her chin to her chest at hearing those words, then looked up at her parents and said, "Yes, I know— grown up talk again. Okay, but we can still go sailing today and have a picnic, can't we?

Dietrich replied, "We'll see after we have breakfast and talk with Aunt Carolyn and Uncle Christopher. Okay?"

"Okaaay," Kira Ann said as she drawled the word out.

After Kira Ann had grabbed up her clothes and bathroom kit she disappeared into the bathroom and they soon heard the shower.

That was the signal for Natalie to quickly tell Lauren a shortened version of their adventurous honeymoon and what happened at New Orleans and of the dark man with the green eyes.

After Natalie had told Lauren the summarized version, Lauren whistled and said, "Wow, that's just like a Hollywood movie but only better! If they ever make that movie, I want to play your part!"

Dietrich looked at Lauren and said, "Could we take a look at the picture you took of the two guys you saw on the boat?"

Lauren replied, "Certainly," and opened her photos app. When the photograph appeared on the screen of Lauren's iPhone, she showed it to Natalie and Dietrich.

Natalie gasped and then held her hand over her mouth and said, "Can you enlarge the picture of the man with the binoculars where we can see his face?"

Lauren quickly enlarged the photo with a quick opening move of her fingers. As the face of the man with the green eyes appeared, Natalie broke out in tears and put her arms around Dietrich while she buried her face against Dietrich's chest and sobbed, "It's him—it's that awful guy with the green eyes that grabbed me and tried to kidnap me at that discotheque, the Masquerade Club at Harrah's Hotel and Casino, when we were in New Orleans!"

"You're kidding aren't you?"

"No! It's him! I could never forget his face and those staring green eyes that have haunted me ever since that incident."

About that time, Kira Ann opened the door of the steamy bathroom and entered the bedroom. She had neatly folded her pajamas and held them over her arm. She was dressed in her walking clothes and shoes, and when she noticed that her mother was wiping some tears from her eyes, she briskly walked over to her and said, "Are you okay?"

Natalie reached down and caressed her glowing face and told her, "Yes, I just got something in my eye and was wiping it away." And then she smiled at her daughter and kissed her on the forehead.

Lauren walked over to Kira Ann and took her by the hand and said to Natalie and Dietrich, "Why don't the two of you go ahead and get dressed while Kira Ann and I go see what her Aunty Carolyn has fixed for us for breakfast?"

Kira Ann smiled at her parents as she and Lauren left the bedroom and walked over to the kitchen where Carolyn was just getting things together for the morning breakfast. She was waiting for the two maids to arrive.

Carolyn looked at Kira Ann and Lauren and said, "You two are certainly early birds. Christopher hasn't even gotten out of bed yet. I'll pour you both some orange juice and then join you out on the porch as soon as the maids arrive."

She opened the refrigerator, took out the orange juice and poured three glasses of orange juice and put them on the kitchen's island cabinet table.

Lauren looked at Carolyn and smiled and then raised her eyes and eyebrows to indicate that she had something to tell her. Carolyn immediately knew something was up and turned to Kira Ann, gave her a glass of orange juice, and softly told her to take the glass and pick out a table on the porch for the three of them.

Kira Ann nodded her head and said, "Okay, I will." Then she took her glass and started walking toward the living room and porch. Just before she left the kitchen, she turned, smiled, and said to both of them, "I know, grown up girl talk," and left to find a porch table.

When Kira Ann had left the kitchen, Lauren told Carolyn the full story about what had happened half an hour ago on the porch and what Natalie had told her about the incident in New Orleans.

Carolyn looked stunned and said, "I remember that incident very well. It scared me half to death when it happened. So, that guy has escaped! I wonder why he's here now and probably with some more of his gang. More Muslim Brotherhood guys, I'll guess. Does this have anything to do with those murders and that attempted kidnapping up in Halifax?"

The two of them had not noticed that Allen had quietly entered the kitchen and had been standing to the side of the door from the hallway next to the kitchen and had heard the whole story as his daughter had related it to Carolyn.

Allen cleared his throat, startling Lauren and Carolyn, who both turned as Allen pronounced, "I'm afraid it is. They're after the treasure and they don't mind what they have to do to accomplish their goal. They have no qualms about killing all of us or selling all of us, including Kira Ann, into slavery or worse!"

14 A STRUGGLE AT SEA

After breakfast, everyone gathered outside on the porch and Christopher decided to tell everyone about the incident that occurred that morning.

Lauren, Natalie and Carolyn decided they would take Kira Ann for a stroll in the backyard garden so she would not hear what Christopher was explaining to everyone on the front porch. Allen decided to join them and distract Kira Ann by telling her about the stories he had heard from his parents about the large golden fish that the Mandarin emperors in ancient China had in their gardens at the Forbidden City Imperial Palace in central Beijing, China, from the Ming dynasty to the Qing dynasty—roughly the years from 1420 to 1912. The Forbidden City served as the home of the Emperors and their households for almost 500 years.

After Allen had told the story about the golden fish, he took Kira by the hand and walked her over to the rock-rimmed pond with a waterfall and water lilies floating on the surface.

"Look there!" as he pointed to a large golden carp lazily swimming among the water lilies.

Kira Ann bent over the edge of the pond to see what Allen was pointing at.

"Oh," she exclaimed. "How pretty. Did Aunty Carolyn get the fish from China?"

Allen replied that the fish also grew in the United States and that the fish in the pond were grown domestically. Allen didn't say anything about American laws concerning bringing plants and animals into the United States.

Kira Ann said, "Oh, that's too bad."

Allen looked at Kira and said, "You know that your name, Kira, means Light or *Star* in Chinese."

Kira looked at Allen with big eyes and replied, "That's what it means in the Czech Republic where mommy grew up."

By this time, Lauren, Natalie and Carolyn had joined Allen and Kira just in time to hear Kira Ann talk about her mother's childhood in the Czech Republic.

Carolyn remarked, "Kira is such a pretty name for a pretty girl." And then she turned to Natalie and said, "I forget how you said she got her middle name of Ann?"

Natalie answered, "Ann Elliott, or Annie as we call her, was the farm woman who saved Dietrich's life at Saint Mary Chapel and the Thirteen Sycamores in Scotland. She and her husband, Sam, along with their children Susan and Brian, live in the farmhouse across the road from the chapel. Annie and Sam are Kira Ann's Godparents."

"Oh, yes, now I remember. That was quite a honeymoon you and Dietrich had. Christopher and I will certainly never forget it!"

Carolyn turned to Lauren and Allen and said, "You'll have to have Natalie and Dietrich tell you all about it."

Kira Ann was taking all of this in and looked up toward her mother and said, "When will you tell me?"

Natalie picked up Kira Ann and kissed her on her cheek and whispered, "When you're a little older."

Kira Ann laid her head on her mother's shoulder and sighed, "You're always telling me that."

Meanwhile, on the porch, Christopher relayed all that had happened that morning to the rest of their guests who listened intently.

When Christopher finished with his narrative, he asked if anyone had any questions.

John Zachary raised his hand and said, "I don't quite understand this thing about the Arab with the green eyes and how he fits into this picture. I presume that this faction of the Muslim Brotherhood in the United States is after something we are after, but why would he have so much hatred in his heart for us?"

Lauren and Allen had just walked onto the porch when they heard John Zachary Bartholomew's question.

Christopher looked at Zach and said, "Well, I think he has a hatred for all nonbelievers, but especially Westerners. It all stems back to the beginning of our quest for answers to the questions we had about the Knights Templar treasure and Mohammad al Hussaini and his hatred for Dietrich because he was the leader of a Luftwaffe squadron that destroyed his team of terrorists in Afghanistan when they were planting IEDs along a road in Kandahar Province.

During that raid Mohammad was left for dead but survived his ordeal and later found out in Germany that Dietrich was the leader of that squadron. He planned to take out his revenge against Dietrich by killing both Dietrich and his wife Natalie.

He continued saying that he had left the kidnapping of Natalie up to his son Ahmed Ali and the Arab with the green eyes, Mustafa. Mustafa had been promised that if he did not kill Natalie he could have her as his slave to do with as he might choose."

He continued, "When Mustafa and his two accomplices tried to kidnap Natalie in the crowded discotheque, Masquerade in New Orleans, Dietrich and I were there to stop them."

They didn't know how tough we were. I was Texas state champion in martial arts, and Dietrich was overpoweringly surged with adrenaline when they attempted the kidnapping. I'm afraid I broke a couple of Mustafa's ribs, and Dietrich broke some noses. We sent them to the hospital. The would-be assailants were arrested by Federal authorities, but I heard later that Mustafa had been repatriated back to Saudi Arabia from Guantanamo Bay.

Lauren's ears perked up when she heard that Christopher was a martial arts champion since she also was a martial arts champion—a Black Belt in Tae Kwon Do.

There was a slight ripple of chuckling when Christopher described how he and Dietrich had stopped the attempted kidnapping.

Christopher continued, "Carolyn and I had planned on taking everyone on a picnic cruise of Mobile Bay, but under the circumstances, I think Dietrich and I should drive over to the Coast Guard Aviation Training Center in Mobile and alert them about the O'Day 23 sloop. The ATC flies the Sikorsky MH-60 Jayhawk helicopters and could easily keep an eye on them."

He added, "I think on the way back we'll drop by the Fairhope Docks Marina and Yacht Club to check on *The Columbine*.

After the discussion, Natalie, Carolyn and Kira Ann walked onto the porch and Carolyn announced they were going to have a pleasant smorgasbord and hors d'oeuvres with drinks in the patio garden in the backyard.

Lauren and Allen sauntered over to Christopher and Allen said, "Would it be okay for us to go with you when you go to the Coast Guard Station and then to the marina to check out your boat? Lauren has a 55-foot sloop at the Marina Del Rey in Los Angeles.

Christopher looked at Lauren and smiled. He then asked her, "Now let me get this straight. You are a Black Belt Tae Kwon Do, you sail a boat in the Catalina Straits, and you are an actress and a mind reader?"

She laughed and said, "Among other things. I've sailed to Hawaii, down to Peru, and won a few races with a selected crew, but I've never been on board a Hinckley Bermuda 50."

Christopher smiled and then declared as he looked at Dietrich, "I think we have a new captain on board! Captain Lauren, would you like to do a short shakedown cruise this afternoon on your new command?"

Lauren was stunned and then stammered, "Yes sir!"

And then she looked at her father and said, "Pops, you're not frightened are you?"

"Of course not. Don't you remember that I was your communications officer and navigator—well sort of," as he corrected himself and continued, "On your trip to Peru?"

They all laughed and then the four crew comrades walked together to the back patio.

Dietrich whispered to Lauren, "Captain, I think we better hurry before the wolves eat all of the food."

"Aye, aye mate!" Lauren laughed.

During the luncheon, Natalie was talking with Lauren and Allen and they mentioned to her that Christopher and Dietrich were going to take Lauren and him with them to the Coast Guard ATC and then to the Marina to do a shakedown cruise.

Natalie responded, "That's great. I think I would like to go along."

Dietrich had wandered over to them and overheard Natalie say that she wanted to go along for the ride.

Dietrich looked into her hazel eyes and said, "Are you sure darling? You were pretty shook up this morning."

"Yeah! I'm okay this morning. I doubt if we'll see those jokers again. Lauren probably scared them off. Besides it's a big bay."

Lauren told her about her boat, *Nic & Dime* and that she had skippered a cruise to Hawaii and Peru and her father had been the Communications and Navigation officer on those trips.

Natalie mentioned to Lauren that she had heard that she was a Tae Kwon Do Black Belt champion and was a sailor. She told Lauren that they had a lot in common in martial arts and sailing. She added that she had also been a skipper in a few championship races and won a couple of cups when she was younger.

The two of them continued talking about their mutual interest in sailing and martial arts. Natalie told her also how she and Christopher had dealt with another attempted kidnapping by the Muslim Brotherhood in Corpus Christi and how Dietrich and Randall had disposed of their tormentors in Austin, Texas, at a football game.

Lauren was astounded at the story. Natalie told her that all of this had happened on their honeymoon after the incident at the thirteen sycamores.

Lauren asked, "Where were the police when this happened?"

Natalie replied, "Oh, Dietrich and Randall had Lieutenant Robert Stewart of the Texas Rangers with them so everything was official. They had been deputized by the Rangers."

Randall's shots were amazing. And then she added, "You know that Dietrich, Christopher, and I are expert with a pistol or rifle!"

Lauren stammered, "Do you have a carry license?"

"Yes, we both do. You know Dietrich and I are in the military; well, Dietrich is a colonel in the German Air Force and we have to travel a lot. After our honeymoon, Dietrich insisted that I learn how to defend myself. When Kira Ann is old enough, we'll make sure she can defend herself. It's a must in today's age when so much is going on around the world."

Lauren was stunned. She had studied the martial arts, but not how to use guns. She was scared of them.

Natalie continued, "You know if you sail in the Mediterranean, the Indian Ocean or around some of the Pacific Islands or even in the Caribbean, you should have a registered firearm on board in case you encounter any pirates."

Lauren gasped at the word PIRATES, "I guess I've been in safer waters."

Natalie countered, "If you've sailed off the coast of Mexico or South America, you haven't. Those waters have become less tame in recent years because of all the drug smuggling."

The luncheon went rapidly and it was time for Natalie, Lauren, Allen, Dietrich and Christopher to drive to the Coast Guard Station in Mobile. It didn't take long to talk to the commanding officer, who Carolyn and Christopher had met at a public charity concert in Fairhope. Christopher explained what had happened that morning and about their concerns. The commander, Captain Jones, told them that he would have one of the helicopter crews make a flyover to be sure they checked out the O'Day 23 and make sure everything was okay. Satisfied, Lauren and her crew drove to the Fairhope Docks Marina to look at *The Columbine*.

It was about three o'clock in the afternoon when the Bermuda 50 Hinckley sloop, *The Columbine*, pulled away from its nesting berth at Fairhope Docks Marina and Yacht Club north of Fairhope, Alabama. The draft of the boat with the center keel board up was seven feet and 11-1/2 feet with the keel board down, allowing good sailing in shallow or deep water. It was wide-beamed at 14 feet 3 inches with an overall length of 49 feet 10 inches. The cabin had a galley, two dining areas accommodating seven people and a bathroom with shower. The large table and seating area could be converted to a bed. The forward bedroom had a queen sized bed with a small bathroom and shower. The aft deck had two large benches, one on either side with an open stern to facilitate swimming, diving or water skiing. The large main sail was rigged for fast tacking and maneuverability.

Christopher had decided that his new skipper should first cruise the mouth of the bay so they could see where it was that Admiral David Farragut had once uttered his order at the Battle of Mobile Bay during the Civil War, "Damn the torpedoes, full speed ahead."

After that they were going to sail the full length of the bay back to the marina and drive home to Cliff House.

Lauren had looked the boat over thoroughly after they had boarded. The boat had received its seaworthy and safety certification which Christopher kept secure in the forward bedroom. Lauren and Allen with Natalie, Dietrich and Christopher watching, had checked out the engine, the radio and communications equipment, and tuned the radio to the harbor police frequency in case of any emergency. Christopher had placed his Dawson Precision Practical Advantage .40

caliber pistol with its large capacity magazine in a drawer of a bedside cabinet in the bedroom as he always did just in case of emergency.

The incident that morning had pretty well shaken everybody now that they realized they were now being surveilled by the Muslim Brotherhood again.

The weather and sea breezes coming from the Gulf permitted them to use minimum tacking and fairly long reaches. They made it back to the vicinity of the white sandy beach with the Ecor Rouge on the left and Cliff House dead ahead. That's when Christopher spotted the O'Day 23 still anchored where Lauren had seen it earlier that morning.

Christopher had his zoom binoculars around his neck, and after he pulled the binoculars up to his eyes, he could see the two dark swarthy Arabs looking toward Cliff House.

They had blindsided the intruders!

Lauren had noticed them as well and said to Christopher, "Do you think we should approach them and try to talk to them?"

"No, I think we should call the harbor police and the Coast Guard and let them know what is happening and that we are going to try and block them from leaving."

Lauren turned to her father and asked him to get on the radio and tell the harbor police and the Coast Guard what was happening.

She was already approaching them swiftly from the south and had Dietrich lower the main sail while Natalie lowered the jib. They were coasting toward the O'Day 23 with Lauren tacking to come within hailing distance.

Allen had immediately complied and was soon on the radio talking to the police and giving them their location and what was happening. No sooner had Natalie furled the jib and Dietrich had dropped the sand anchor to halt their boat, a shot rang out from the O'Day 23, narrowly missing Lauren. She ducked and screamed.

Allen heard her scream and told the police that the two Arabs had fired on them with a gun and narrowly missed his daughter.

Natalie had remembered Christopher's pistol and ran inside the cabin to the bedroom to get it. She opened the drawer to the bedside cabinet, withdrew the pistol and, without closing the drawer, ran through the cabin door and back on deck when another shot rang out and hit the cabin, shattering a window. Natalie reached the deck railing and saw the man with the green eyes getting ready to fire again. She leveled her gun and fired. The .40 caliber anti-personnel slug screamed through the air and hit its mark, shattering the Arab's right shoulder and causing him to drop his pistol into the water. She heard him scream as the impact of the bullet knocked him back onto the deck of his sloop.

Suddenly, a police helicopter appeared overhead with a swat policeman hanging out of the helicopter's door, leveling his M-4 carbine at the two men and shouting to the Arab and his wounded comrade to lie face down on the deck and not to move. Fifteen minutes later a police harbor boat pulled alongside the O'Day 23 sloop and took the two Arabs into custody.

Natalie was standing next to the cabin door of *The Columbine*. She was still holding Christopher's pistol in her right hand and had an angry look on her face.

Christopher walked over to her and gently reached for his pistol as he said, "Don't you think I should put that thing away?"

She handed the gun to him and said firmly, "I missed, I aimed for his heart!"

Lauren, who was standing next to her father, whispered into his ear, "Damn, I wouldn't want that lady to be angry with me!"

No one noticed the angry young man with black shaggy hair and a swarthy complexion who had been watching with binoculars the confrontation at sea of Natalie and her tormentor with the green eyes. His eyes were also green and he was standing at the end of the fishing and observation pier that jutted seventy-five yards out into Mobile Bay from the beach just below the cliff in front of Cliff House. He had just witnessed his twin brother and his accomplice being arrested by the harbor police.

No one knew the three men were members of the Muslim Brotherhood and had planned that night on capturing and kidnapping everyone at Cliff House and taking them to a larger ship waiting patiently off the barrier islands to receive the captives. Their intent was to drug them and take them to the Dutch island of Curaçao where they would be transported by private airplane to the Middle East and sold as slaves!

15 NEW ENGLAND

The shock of the battle at sea in front of Cliff House had caused quite a stir in the neighborhood. No one who had witnessed the encounter had seen anything like it. Rumors quickly started circulating that the police had broken up a fight involving the arrest and capture of some drug smugglers who had been caught red-handed by a Fairhope citizen, one of their neighbors, and that one of the smugglers had been wounded trying to escape during the encounter with a vigilant citizen of Fairhope, but the names were not being released.

Some said it was a woman who returned fire with deadly accuracy when she was fired upon by one of the smugglers as they were trying to escape and that her boat had blocked their escape.

Everyone back at Cliff House unanimously agreed that it was time to return home and let the rumors run their course. It would be better, if worse came to worse, that Carolyn and Christopher should be recognized as breaking up a criminal element that was trying to invade their community.

John Zachary Bartholomew was more than willing not to complicate his position at the University of Florida and draw attention to the company of fellow historians and treasure seekers.

Lauren and Allen were perfectly comfortable to move the location of their pursuit of the treasure to New England where they all believed the treasure to be hidden—but where? They had more than enough clues—maybe too many! Lauren postulated they were looking at the solution to the puzzle but couldn't see it because it was too simple and staring them in the face.

During their meeting in Fairhope, all of the pieces of the puzzle had been put before them, but which ones applied and which ones were merely filler pieces not contributing to the picture?

Natalie and Dietrich felt they were too close to their objective to return to Alamogordo and could leave Kira Ann with Mary K., Matt, and Daisy. Randall wanted to be in on the finding of the treasure, and Carolyn and Christopher eventually would have to get back to Texas and the University of Texas Medical Center in San Antonio. Randall, Natalie, Dietrich and Allen were on a month leave, and Lauren was between gigs so they all had time to go to New England and camp out in Boston close to all of the main clues.

The decision was made by the *Adventurers*, as they called themselves, to make their headquarters in Boston.

Randall mused, "Hmmm, that's what the Pilgrims called themselves when they decided to seek their place under the sun in the New World!"

The Revere Hotel near the Boston Commons was decided upon by the adventurers to be their headquarters as they explored the various places in New England and look for the possible clues that might be the key to finding the treasure that Prince Henry had secreted so long ago. Randall, Natalie and Dietrich, Lauren, and Allen decided to make a list of the various clues that had been left around New England.

They traveled from George Bush Houston International Airport to Boston's Logan International Airport without any difficulty or delays and arrived right on schedule.

They had rented a Mercedes GLE 550e plug-in hybrid SUV having 4MATIC drive with up to 50 mpg on an electric drive with turbo quickness from a Boston dealer. The dealer had the SUV waiting for them when they arrived at Boston's Logan International Airport. The dealer had a driver meet them with the rented SUV, who promptly acquainted them with the specifics of the new car and then asked who was going to drive the auto.

Lauren volunteered, so he let her slide behind the wheel and he took his place in the forward passenger seat and they drove away for a ten minute drive to check her driving skills. When they returned, the driver announced that Lauren was not only an excellent driver but could probably qualify to drive one of their sports race cars.

Lauren beamed with pride at his remarks, they all loaded their luggage into the back of the vehicle, and Lauren drove them to the Revere Hotel using the on-board GPS.

They all checked into the hotel and went directly to their rooms which were located together and promptly unpacked their clothes and belongings. They took about thirty minutes to refresh before going to Randall's suite where he had ordered a late lunch for everyone.

They had had already decided that Oak Island just off the coast of Nova Scotia had been one of the places the Vikings and Prince Henry had probably visited. The mysterious well that had been placed there and so ingeniously constructed was no doubt the work of the Templars and Cistercians. It has been excavated over the last two centuries by treasure-seekers to no avail, so they could eliminate it as an area to search for clues.

Randall explained to everyone, "From the late 1700s there has been speculation about treasure being buried on Oak Island. In the summer of 1795, a teenaged boy by the name of Daniel McGinnis saw strange lights at night on the small island off shore from his house on the mainland.

"When he investigated the island the next day, he noticed a strange circular depression in the ground in a clearing where a number of oak trees had been cut down years ago. Above that clearing approximately thirteen feet in diameter, a lone oak tree with a sawed off limb which hung directly over the depression had a block and tackle which hung from the limb directly over the hole.

"Upon seeing this, he excitedly returned to the mainland with a tale of possible pirate's treasure. He enlisted the aid of two of his friends, Anthony Vaughan and John Smith, and the next day the three boys rowed over to the island and began their excavations of the depression. It was well known to the inhabitants of the area that pirates had frequented the area as a refuge after preying upon the commercial ships going to and leaving the busy port of Boston just 200 nautical miles south of Oak Island. One infamous pirate, Captain Kidd, bragged about burying some of his treasure in an unspecified area around Oak Island before his capture in 1699.

"Two feet beneath the topsoil, the boys found a carefully constructed rock floor which they removed and continued as the hole shrunk from 13 feet to 7 feet in diameter. At ten feet they discovered a partially decomposed floor of wood. Upon striking the wooden floor, they heard a hollow sound indicating a chamber, but on removing the floor, all they saw was an empty chamber with a clay floor. Discouraged and believing that the strange lights that Daniel McGinnis saw were from the pirates who had returned and retrieved their treasure, the boys went home. After a few weeks of thinking about it and not understanding why if they had, indeed, removed the treasure would they take the time to fill the hole back up and leave two floors, one of stone and the other of wood, which obviously had been in place for a long time.

"The boys returned to the pit they had dug and continued their excavation. After they had dug another ten feet they encountered another wooden floor," and after removing that floor, they dug five feet more into the hard clay and decided to give up.

"Over the years, many fortune-seekers have been attracted to the lure of treasure suggested by the Oak Island excavations. In 1804, after finding a layer of coconut fibers at sixty feet which has been used over the centuries as packing for precious items being transported, and two more additional timber floors followed by hollow chambers, a large heavy square-cut stone tablet was discovered at ninety feet with an enigmatic inscription of strange symbols. Each character of the mysterious text was a singular combination of arrows, dots, and lines, much like the type of symbols the Knights Templar might have used.

"There have been many attempts to decipher the encoded script, and in the 1860s Professor James Leitchi of Dalhousie University, after using a simple substitution cipher technique, declared that the message on the stone said, "Forty feet below, two million pounds are buried!" Many question this translation since pounds is a description of English currency, and the Vikings or Templars would have described it as gold, silver, etc., rather than a certain specific currency. Some have said it was meant to be the weight of the treasure, but again the term is English, or perhaps the professor just translated the weight from a Nordic language term into English.

"At any rate, although particles of gold dust, part of a gold chain, old copper coins, a lead cross, and a piece of ancient parchment with the Roman numeral VI written on it with ancient iron ball ink, many people have tried to unravel the secret of Oak Island. Even John Wayne, Errol Flynn and Franklin Delano Roosevelt, to name a few, have sought the treasure. With the lure of finding untold treasure in their hearts, these seekers, using many different excavation techniques and vast sums of money, have still not found the treasure. Oak Island is a mystery yet to be solved."

Lauren thought about what Randall had just said and remarked, "Well, let's make a list of potential clues and their places and work out a schedule to visit them and see what we might find."

They all agreed and after eating the lunch that had been served to the room, they sat down around the conference table and began to make out the list of places to visit and their timetable.

Allen began the discussion by saying, "We have all been to Fairhope and looked at the evidence of Welsh explorations there and the Welsh claims that Prince Madoc ab Owain Gwynedd was the true discoverer of Mobile Bay and is reputed to have made three voyages across the Atlantic Ocean: The first to reconnoiter an ocean passage from Ireland using the great circle route of the Vikings down the east coast and around Florida and the Keys to the Gulf Coast areas.

"According to the 1584 *History of Cambria*, he and his brother, Rhirid, set sail with 100 settlers on his second voyage where they encountered the Choctaw, Mobiles, Natchez, and Caddos Indians around the mouth and delta areas of the Mississippi River. The Natchez, Choctaw, and Caddos Indians were allies of the Aztecs who controlled the trade and commerce of the Gulf Coast area. It was from these fierce tribes that Prince Madoc and his brother learned of the more peaceful Chicasaw, Creek, Cherokee, and Mobile Indians and discover the Ecor Rouge navigational marker where the Mobile Indians lived. In the Mobile area he saw the opportunity where he could settle more Welsh and Irish settlers for his new colony he could develop for the Templars.

Prince Madoc and his brother Rhirid were Templars and his father had sired several claimants to his throne in Wales. His peaceful and pious nature forced him to leave Wales when his other brothers began a feud resulting in an internecine war after his father's death. He had anticipated what would happen when his father died and thus began his search for a new kingdom. He knew of Leif Erikson's voyages and was determined to follow his path. So, after finding an ideal spot in Mobile Bay, he returned home to recruit more disgruntled fair-haired and blue-eyed Irish and Welsh settlers for his new kingdom. He left his brother Rhirid in charge of the settlers and promised them he would return with more.

"With the aid of the Templars and their need for expansion, he soon found enough settlers to form a fleet of ten ships carrying settlers, soldiers, cattle, and farm animals. He had not heard of the buffalo that roamed North America from coast to coast until after he had arrived with his fleet and settlers in 1170."

Allen continued, "The Welsh and Irish settlers were later forced north by the Choctaw and Seminole Indians following the Alabama and Coosa Rivers to the southern part of the Appalachian Mountain Plateau into Northern Georgia and Chattanooga area of Tennessee and then to their fortified island below the Ohio Falls. There a massive battle occurred resulting in the deaths of thousands of the Indians and the white tribe of Welsh and Irish heritage who escaped down the Ohio River to the Mississippi-Missouri Rivers and up the Missouri River where they intermarried and became the Mandan Indians of Sacajawea fame only to succumb and die out after the smallpox epidemic of 1837-38.

"In 1832, the artist George Catlan visited the Mandans near Fort Clark and painted the Mandans and drew scenes of Mandan life and portraits of chiefs. George Catlin, like members of the Lewis and Clark expedition, believed the Mandans were the white Indians of folklore, the descendants of Prince Madoc and his followers.

"Hjalmar Holand had proposed that breeding with the Norse, Irish, and Welsh survivors of the 'Great Battle' of Ohio Falls might explain the blond Indians among the Mandan on the upper Missouri River."

Dietrich postulated that DNA taken from the teeth of the still existent skeletons of the Great Battle of the Ohio Falls and of the skeletons of known Mandan Indians of the upper Missouri River might be possible since viable DNA has been taken from the teeth of mastodon as well as Egyptian mummies and even dinosaurs.

After Allen finished his points, Lauren remarked, "If all of this is true, then the markers in New England probably would be the place to start. What is the closest clue, and then we can just follow them until we find the answer to the puzzle— right!"

Dietrich spoke up, "Right! Let's start with the Westford Knight and Boatstone in Westford, Massachusetts, since it is nearby, then we can visit the Narragansett rüne stone located near Pojac Point on Narragansett Bay, and across the bay to the Newport stone tower in Newport, Rhode Island, since it appears to be constructed the same as the towers in Alabama and Georgia. The foundation stones of the fort and tower on the island in the Ohio River below the Ohio Falls appears to suggest they are all of the same style of construction found in Scotland, Wales, and Ireland. Even the Cambridge Round Church in Cambridge, England, and the 1150 AD Eynhallow Church in Orkney, Scotland, resemble the towers found in America.

16 WESTFORD

The morning sky was bright and an anticipation of new discovery and the possible vital clues that our adventurers needed to put all the parts of the puzzle together filled their thoughts. Everyone was anticipating a possible solution. They all gathered for a breakfast buffet with made-to-order buttery croissants and yogurt parfaits. After eating a hearty breakfast they went to their rooms, and after getting their gear together, they rendezvoused in Randall's suite.

Everyone was prompt and Lauren was asking her father whether she should go back to her room and get an umbrella in case of rain. She had heard the weather was unpredictable in Boston and didn't want to be caught in a sudden shower. She wasn't sure but when she looked it up on her iPhone, she saw it was only 35 miles and took about 45 minutes to drive if it wasn't during morning or evening commuting hours. She decided that she better return to her room and get her umbrella.

Just after she left, the telephone in Randall's room rang and an old familiar voice spoke to him. It was Steve Grant from the Scottish branch of police for homeland security that handled terrorism in Scotland.

"Hello, Steve is that you," and without waiting for an answer, Randall continued, "What's up?"

Steve explained they had intercepted a communication from Jeddah, Saudi Arabia, behind the Crescent Curtain to a Muslim Brotherhood leader in Scotland advising him that the Muslim Brotherhood leader in the United States had been shot in his right shoulder and, along with his second in command, was arrested by the Fairhope, Alabama, police. Apparently, the Muslim Brotherhood was reassigning one of its leaders in Scotland to go to the United States and take charge of its U.S. branch and eliminate or abduct the woman who shot him, as well as anyone, including her husband and family or friends, who got in their way.

Steve continued to say that he found out from MI-5 that Natalie was the woman who shot the terrorist and that he was the one who had tried to kidnap her a little more than six years ago in New Orleans. He said he also knew that Carolyn and Christopher had a house in Fairhope. He said he called Christopher and told him the whole story and that Kira Ann was in Texas at Randall's Back Forty Ranch with Mrs. Stuart and Matt. The Texas Rangers were alerted, and they sent Bob Stewart out to the ranch to inform Mary K. Stuart and put a Ranger on the ranch as security.

Steve continued, "It's amazing, I thought that the guy with the green eyes, Mustafa, was in Guantanamo?"

"Yeah, he was, but he was released to Saudi Arabia," replied Randall.

Steve said, "He must have worked his way back to the U.S. over your southern border and then tracked Natalie and Dietrich to Fairhope. I guess it was when he was ordered to clear up the bungling in Halifax that he knew he should shadow Natalie and Dietrich since he knew Dietrich had been the impetus for the Templar treasure search in the first place. And besides, Dietrich was a knight in the Hospitaller Order of Saint John which automatically made him an enemy of the Muslim Brotherhood since he was a member of a Crusading Order!"

Randall thought that over for a minute and then said, "I guess you are notifying me that we should all be careful, and we might be in danger."

"Yes, and also your friend Allen and his daughter, Lauren."

"You know about them!"

"Well, we actually were told about them and about what all of you are doing in Boston by the Mossad."

There was silence on the telephone and then, Randall asked, "Is this call in the open? How can you tell me these things without a scrambled phone?"

"Oh, we're way beyond scrambling phones now, but I can't tell you. The Mossad knew the whereabouts of Mustafa before your government or ours knew. They are two steps ahead of everybody. Their very existence depends on it!" replied Steve.

Then Steve added, "Don't alarm anyone, but you have a friendly shadow as well as an evil one, only the evil shadow doesn't know it."

The phone clicked and Randall stood there silently with the phone still to his ear when Dietrich shook his shoulder and said, "What did Steve want?"

"He just wanted to know how everyone is doing and that he had heard from Christopher that we were all in Boston at the Revere Hotel and just wanted to say hello."

Dietrich pressed him, "It's more than that, isn't it?"

"Yes, it's New Orleans, Corpus Christi, Austin, and the Rose Garden all rolled up into one with all the same players and whatever necessary substitutes."

By this time, Natalie had moved over to Dietrich and was listening to the conversation with great intent.

"It's beginning again, isn't it?"

Dietrich put his arm around his wife's waist and whispered, "Yes, and the angels from the River Jordan are over our shoulders again."

"Thank God!" replied Natalie. "Is it Ari Shapiro?"

"I hope so."

Allen had been standing next to his daughter, Lauren, and whispered into her ear, "What was that all about?"

Lauren replied, "Steve, his friend from Scotland security, just said that the Muslim Brotherhood is onto us looking for the Templar treasure, that they are watching everything we do, and the Israeli intelligence and security service, the Mossad, is watching them and us, and that Natalie hopes it is the same Mossad agent that was looking after them in Europe who is here in the United States now."

Allen replied, "I didn't hear that."

Lauren answered, "You weren't really using your eyes and ears, just your ears. Didn't you notice the change in both Natalie's, Dietrich's and Randall's posture and facial expressions and different tones of speech?

"We are clearly in danger with these madmen. I wish we were in Texas and had a gun, but we're in Massachusetts and going to Rhode Island where we can't pack heat."

Allen looked startled and stammered, "Where did you learn to speak like that?"

"Oh, pops, I learned it from a television series I appeared in," she replied.

Allen looked over to Randall and said, "I guess I'm still in the Twentieth Century."

Randall looked knowingly to his colleague and friend and replied, "If that's the case, I must be in the Nineteenth Century," and then he grinned and started laughing, which made Allen start to laugh.

Lauren looked quizzically at her father and his friend and said, "What are you two laughing at?"

Allen looked at her and said, "One day, you'll know."

Dietrich broke the ice and said, "Well, I guess we better get over to Westford and take a look at the boat stone and the knight."

They put on light coats and left Randall's apartment and went down to the garage where their SUV was parked. They unlocked the doors and settled into their comfortable seats. Lauren was driving and her father was riding shotgun in the front passenger seat. The trip to Westford was smooth and relatively quick with Lauren using the GPS to reach their destination, the J.V. Fletcher Library in Westford. In the library was a stone found near an area thought to be the winter camp of the Saint Clair expedition. The 200- to 300-pound glacial granite boulder, known as the Westford Boat Stone had been unearthed by a local farmer, William Wyman, in 1932. The carvings on the stone were certainly ancient and in the fashion used by the Cistercian monks on Göttland.

One of the carvings on the stone showed a ship with a single mast bearing two square sails. On the upper part of the hull of the ship are eight ports for oars. Another carving showed a vertical arrow with four pairs of feathers in Nordic style, rather than Indian style. A third carving showed what appeared to be the number 184 with the upper part of the loop forming the eight open like the astrological symbol for Taurus—a large prominent constellation in the Northern Hemisphere's winter sky—which means it is crossed by the plane of the ecliptic.

The third number, an open four, is the astrological symbol for the planet Jupiter seen in the direction south along the ecliptic of the winter sky. In other words, it could be the marker stone where Prince Henry anchored his boat at the foot of a hill in deep enough water where he could moor his ships for the winter.

The number appears to be an astrological code indicating that he had sailed from the north and wintered at a safe harbor, and the arrow was pointing south to where he would sail after the winter. Approximately 600 yards away from the location of the boat stone were stones laid out like the foundations of three stone enclosures similar to Viking stone buildings in Greenland known as storehouses.

The effigy known as the Westford Knight lies approximately four blocks from the library on an outcrop of bedrock next to a well-traveled road. There is a chain fence supported by five stone columns that clearly shows the outline of a medieval knight in full mail and armor holding a Scottish broadsword and armorial shield against his breast.

The carving is the representation of a knight holding a

partially broken sword which was the Viking symbol for the death of a warrior. The style of the knight's helmet indicated a date between 1376 and 1400. The armorial bearings on the shield were identified as the armorial bearings of a Clan Gunn chief from Thurso. In other words, it is highly likely that the image is a true medieval memorial carved in North America by a Cistercian monk in the Prince Henry expedition commemorating the death of Earl Henry's closest companion, Sir James Gunn, who is believed to have died during the ascent of nearby Prospect Hill.

Allen remarked that the grave of Sir James Gunn would have been close by the outcropping of stone that carried his image carved in stone. He further stated that this reminded him of the recent finding in September 2012 of the grave of King Richard III under a parking lot covering the ancient site of the former Greyfriars Friary Church in Leicester, England. He went on further to postulate that the remains of Sir James Gunn buried in his armor and with his sword might even be under the nearby road by the outcropping of bedrock bearing his image.

This information completely unnerved the entire group. It certainly indicated that Prince Henry continued south from Massachusetts the very next spring after the death of his Templar friend. But where? They surely must find the answer perhaps in Narragansett Bay which was the next place to visit in their quest. The adventurers were thrilled at what they had seen and heard which made it apparent they were following in Prince Henry and the treasure's footsteps. They were all so giddy with their discoveries, they didn't notice the two swarthy men with black hair and beards sitting in a 2018 black Ford F-150 pickup truck across and down the street from the library where they had parked their Mercedes SUV.

They thanked Mary Smith, the curator of the J.V. Fletcher Library and Museum, and said they appreciated her descriptions and telling the story of the two ancient artifacts they had just seen and their place in the history of America.

As they pulled away from their parking space, they waved

at her and started the 35-mile trip back to their hotel. They did not notice the black pickup truck that began to follow them.

17 BACK TO BOSTON

They had gone about half a mile down Main Street, when Lauren announced, "Hey gang, I think we are being followed by two Middle Eastern guys with beards and mean looks on their faces." She slowed down and asked," Would you all very slowly and not all at once look back and tell me what you think. This doesn't look good!"

Lauren activated the advanced Surround View system of the Mercedes GLE 550e. The system uses cameras in all four directions to compose a single live overhead view of the immediate surroundings. It is displayed on the large in-dash command screen at lower speed maneuvers. She slowed down so everyone could look forward to the large screen which easily showed the two men in the Ford pickup.

The two men had not anticipated Lauren's slowing down so they came closer to the rear of their vehicle, and everyone could clearly see the men in high definition.

Allen took out his iPhone and snapped the men's picture. Dietrich did the same thing and then e-mailed the photo to Steve Grant in Scotland. He hoped Steve was still in his office since it was only 10:30 a.m. in Massachusetts and 4:30 p.m. in Scotland. Immediately, Dietrich's iPhone rang and he was communicating with Steve via FaceTime.

"What's with the two guys in the pickup truck?" Steve asked.

"Steve, could you run an I.D. on those two guys?"

"Sure, but it will take a couple of minutes," was Steve's reply.

"Okay."

Within three minutes Steve was back, and as they talked, Steve said, "Dietrich, those two guys are really bad dudes! One is Abdul Ghaffar Hakim and the other is Burhan al Din Raheem. They were in Edinburgh just two weeks ago, and suddenly they disappeared last week. It looks as though they are on your trail. Be extremely cautious, they have been implicated in some beheadings."

"Okay, thanks, we'll keep in touch," replied Dietrich.

Then Steve added, "Oh, by the way, I've already notified your angels in the CIA and Mossad. They said they were right on your bad boys' case. One of your angels is Ari Shapiro who has been recently assigned to the United States. You may remember how he helped Carolyn and Christopher in their car chase in Marburg."

There was a long pause and then Dietrich replied, "Oh, yes I remember."

Everyone could hear Steve laugh and then say, "Just a second, I'm patching Ari's handsome face and smile into your high definition television communication screen on your Mercedes' dash."

Suddenly, Ari Shapiro's face appeared and he said, "Lauren, don't panic. My partner, David, who your father met in the Rose Garden in Jerusalem and I are right behind your bad guys in a grey Mercedes GLE 550e just like yours, except we are armor plated. Lauren, I want you to take Main Street east and where it forks; then take the left road, Depot Street, where we have arranged a surprise for your friends behind you."

Lauren was wide-eyed and amazed at all of these fast-paced surveillance techniques being used.

She smiled and said, "I didn't know all of this is real. In the movies, it's all make-believe and green screen."

Dietrich looked at Natalie, who was smiling, and then turned back to Lauren and said, "If you think this is something, you should see what the Air Force can do. It's almost out of *Star Trek*."

Suddenly, Steve's voice announced over the Mercedes linked in phone system, "Okay, we have our armored SUVs in place several miles ahead where Lowell Road and Plains Road intersect in a triangle."

Lauren's eyes were wide with wonder and she gasped, "This is real, I'm not acting in a movie, this is real!"

She took a couple of deep breaths and said to Steve, "Roger that!"

Thirty seconds later, Ari was back on the screen and announced, "Lauren, keep calm. When you get to the intersection, I'll let you know when to press your accelerator to the floor so one of our SUVs can fall in behind you and in front of the pickup truck following you. Our second SUV will block any exit by the bad guys onto Lowell Road. After you accelerate down Plains Road, keep going. Our people will close in on your guys in the pickup truck and take care of them. Don't look back, it's going to be just like Sodom and Gomorrah. Go back toward Highway 495 connecting to Highway 93 and back to your hotel in Boston. We'll be with you all the way."

Allen was the first to break the silence, "Lauren, is that the intersection ahead?"

As if Ari and David were inside their vehicle, Ari's image and voice suddenly appeared on the dash video screen and softly said, "Okay, Lauren, you are approaching the triangle intersection. Take the left road and pass our SUV waiting on the right of the triangle intersection. Steady, steady. Okay now press the pedal to the metal and get the hell out of there…. Okay, our SUV is now behind you and in front of the pickup. Good girl, you were perfect. Now get back to Boston!"

Lauren was staring straight ahead as the Mercedes approached 100 miles per hour and the intersection faded from sight.

Suddenly the rear view television kicked on and an image of the distant intersection appeared on the dash television screen. There was a tremendous fireball that erupted at the intersection and a shock wave that shook their Mercedes SUV.

Lauren was grasping the steering wheel with white knuckles, and everyone in their car was stunned by the sight of the fireball on the dash screen.

Allen broke the silence and said, "I guess they resisted arrest and are now with Allah!"

It was an hour and a half later that the five adventurers were back at the Revere Hotel ready to relax and digest the day's adventure in Westford. They quickly parked their SUV and went to their rooms with the understanding they would all meet in the exclusive Rooftop Revere Lounge and Bar for an evening meal with a superb view of Boston.

They each had a suite with a view of Boston. Each suite had a private balcony overlooking the city, a large king size bed with living room, bar, library, and bath with walk in shower. After taking a shower, they met again in Randall's suite where he had ordered some hors d'oeuvres, Glenlivet scotch, and some Dom Perignon champagne.

Allen arrived first, wearing a blue Harris Tweed sport coat with a white oxford shirt and blue and red regimental tie, and black pants and shoes. He was with his daughter, Lauren, who looked smart in a casual canary yellow evening dress with a white silk scarf casually enfolding her shoulders.

Natalie wore a comfortable grey skirt with an ivory silk blouse and blue jacket with a navy blue silk scarf wrapped around her shoulders and dark blue high heels that made her five-foot-eight-inch height almost as tall as Dietrich who was dressed in a white evening jacket, black trousers, white shirt with black tie, and black shoes.

In contrast, Randall wore a brown Harris Tweed jacket with brown leather patches on his elbows and a white button-down collar shirt with a plain brown silk tie and khaki brown pants and brown loafers with scuff marks on his shoes.

The adventurers settled into the chairs and couch in the living room of the suite while their host discussed what drinks were appropriate. The men chose the Glenlivet Scotch, neat of course, and the two ladies who had settled on the couch declared their preference for the champagne.

Lauren had engaged Natalie in a discussion of her adventures and conflict with the man with the green eyes during her honeymoon with Dietrich in Scotland at the Thirteen Sycamores, and in New Orleans where the Muslim Brotherhood and the man with the green eyes had tried to kidnap her. Lauren listened in fascination.

When Natalie told her about her father's part in unraveling the secret of the Holy Grail in the secret Seton family manuscript and his adventures with them in Germany and Jerusalem, Lauren was amazed. She told Natalie that she had no idea that her father had been involved in the solving of the mystery of the Holy Grail. He had never told her about it. She thought he was living a dull professorial life at the University of Texas.

Randall had wandered away from Dietrich and Allen and was casually leaning against the half wall behind the couch, sipping his Scotch and watching the city lights of Boston and the Back Bay. He was thinking about the mystery of the Newport Tower when he overheard Lauren telling Natalie about her life in Hollywood.

She was explaining to Natalie that she thought Hollywood was exciting, but that it was mostly a whirl of auditions, parties to meet influential people that might help her career, and long hours of rehearsals, memorizing lines from a script, honing her acting, dancing and martial arts skills, and putting up with embarrassing sexual harassment from all quarters, and not letting other actors, producers, directors, screenwriters, and talk show hosts know how she really felt about anything.

Randall leaned over and interrupted, "I was under the impression that Hollywood had changed since the late 50s, and that nowadays nothing is the same with all the new technology."

Lauren and Natalie turned to look at Randall, and both had a quizzical look on their faces.

He continued, "From the perspective of an older generation, it seems that both women's and men's everyday dress and physical appearance today looks unwashed, grubby, and almost like hobos and street people. And certainly, the women's dress at the recent Academy Awards looked provocative and most revealing."

Natalie and Lauren were taken aback at Randall's straightforward remarks, and Natalie firmly said, "I think the younger generation—the millennials—would say that it was individual self-expression and following their own path."

"Then why," Randall continued, "do they all look the same? It seems that some dress and hairstyles are an expression of following a certain group, or expression of identity and association with a group for political expression or philosophy. In other words, groupthink, rather than the idea of America being an assimilation and melting pot resulting in a universal and unique American style or persona with individual think."

Natalie paused and as if thinking aloud said, "You mean that individual expression is being subverted into groupthink, and everyone following the party line as they did in communist Russia or used to do in Czechoslovakia when it was under communist control?"

Randall answered, "Exactly! In China, it was following the Little Red Book of Mao and the reeducation of those people who reasoned on their own, solved their own problems, and took individual responsibility for their own actions and wellbeing as is expressed in the American Constitution. In other words, individual freedom."

Natalie thought for a minute, remembering what her parents had told her about her own Jewish grandparents changing their identities and fleeing to Czechoslovakia from Germany and the Nazis, only to be caught in the web of communism there after World War II. She remembered her own experiences growing up in Czechoslovakia and her friend Rania's experiences with the Muslim Brotherhood and their slavish following of the philosophy of Sharia Law and the dictates of the Muslim Brotherhood's fascist leaders and their goal of conquest of the West by immigration, proliferation, and then subjugation!

She nodded her head and said, "I see the dangers of groupthink and the relinquishment of individual freedom of thought and responsibilities to leaders who have only their own agenda and aggrandizement in mind. She remembered her own father's advice to be a leader and not a follower in a mob."

Randall followed up and said to Lauren and Natalie, "After the Constitutional Convention of 1787, Benjamin Franklin was asked by Mrs. Powel of Philadelphia as to what kind of a government the new nation was going to have, and he immediately responded, 'A republic, if you can keep it!'"

Randall then added, "He was right, it's the responsibility of each citizen, not a political party, to keep the republic."

Randall smiled, then turned and walked back to Allen and Dietrich and refilled his glass with the Glenlivet single malt scotch. They were discussing the next day's trip to Newport and the harrowing escape they had that day from the Muslim Brotherhood and wondering why there was so much interest in their expedition.

Natalie and Lauren sat looking at each other and then at Randall who was now suddenly silent and listening to the conversation between Allen and Dietrich.

Lauren was the first to speak and remarked to Natalie, "Dr. Fox certainly has a definite opinion and philosophy about history and the United States. I've never quite heard everything he talked about before."

Then she paused and corrected herself, "Yes, I guess I have. You know, my father and some of our family left China and came to the United States just before China fell to the communists. We still have family in the old country."

Natalie nodded her head and said, "I understand, my family and Dietrich's family are now living in a free Czech Republic and a free Germany, respectively. They know what it was like to not have individual freedom and having to walk and talk the party line like robots."

Lauren added, "Last month, my boyfriend and I watched a couple of movies that were about the party line. They actually were the same story except the 1939 version, *Ninotchka*, with a script by Billy Wilder and directed by Ernst Lubitsch and starring Greta Garbo and Melvin Douglas, was a comedy drama, and the later 1957 Metro Goldwyn Mayer musical screen version, *Silk Stockings*, was an adaptation of the 1955 stage musical of the same name. The movie starred Fred Astaire and Cyd Charisse with Peter Lorre and the music of the Indiana composer Cole Porter.

"I guess the movies pretty much told the same story as to what Randall was trying to say; although, with much more subtlety."

Lauren shrugged her shoulders and said, "I had no idea that my visit with my father between gigs was going to be as exciting and meaningful as it has been thus far."

Natalie laughed and put her arms around Lauren and whispered in her ear, "Real life is not make-believe. Having a family, children and a loving husband is the real adventure in life, and it takes hard work by everyone to keep it."

The men had gathered around the hors d'oeuvres and the Scotch discussing the next part of their quest. Randall noted that it appeared that the next clue to follow was the Newport Tower which was obviously the next step in their search for the path of Prince Henry Saint Clair's fleet. If they traveled south as indicated by the boat stone, they would have had to sail around Cape Cod and then, hugging the shore, sail into Long Island Sound and a safe harbor—Narragansett Bay.

Randall further explained that the elders of the Narragansett Indians have a tradition that states the tower was constructed by "green eyed, fire-haired giants" who came in peace, had a battle, and then left. Architecture professors such as Even Norton Horsford of Harvard University believe the Newport Tower has the shape and form of a baptistery in Scotland that indicates a Viking presence in Newport predating the colonial era by several centuries, which would place it in the timeline of

Prince Henry Saint Clair.

Allen chimed in and remarked how closely the Narragansett Indians describe the white giants the same as the Cherokee traditions of the giant white Indians with blond and red hair with green and blue eyes in Alabama, Florida, Georgia, Tennessee, Kentucky, and Indiana. The Aztec tradition also describes such people. And the stone tower constructions in these Southern and Midwestern states also point to Scandinavian origins.

Allen then read from a book he had brought with him and said, "In 1997, James P. Whittal Jr. of the Early Sites Research Society of Lowell, Massachusetts, who did the most prolonged and dispassionate examination of the Newport Tower wrote:

"The Newport Stone Tower in Newport Rhode Island was constructed in the style of Norman-Romanesque architecture, inspired by the architecture of the Holy Sepulcher in Jerusalem brought back to Europe by returning Crusaders. In its own unique style, the tower was further influenced by a combination of the architecture of temples of the Templars, the round churches of Scandinavia and the local architectural traditions from whence the builders came. Architectural features found in the construction of the tower would date it in the broad range of 1150 to 1400 AD. However, some specific features limit it to a period in the late 1300s. In the course of six years of research I have found the best parallels in the tower's architectural features exist in the Northern Isles of Scotland which were under Norse control during the time frame mentioned. Other features relating the tower to Scandinavian round churches and Templar buildings have been published by Hjalmar R. Holland, Philip A. Means, and F.J. Allen."

Allen looked up from his book and concluded by saying, "James P. Whittal concluded that the tower was at the approximate same latitude of Rome and there were no architectural parallels in colonial New England and suggested that the tower was built as a church, observatory, lighthouse, and a datum zero point for further exploration in the New World. In other words, the tower is where we will find the two clues that Lauren earlier said would break the Gordian knot of this enigma."

Dietrich glanced over to Natalie and noted that she and Lauren were glancing at their watches while looking at the men. He turned to Allen and Randall and suggested that maybe they should think about going to the Rooftop Revere Lounge where they had reservations for dinner.

They looked at their watches and immediately put their glasses down and walked over to Lauren and Natalie and apologized for forgetting about their reservations. The two ladies frowned but forgave them, and they left Randall's suite and went to the Revere Rooftop Lounge.

They got there in time for their reservations, but just barely. They were seated at their table and enjoyed a traditional Boston seafood dinner of lobster and clams, Boston baked beans, baked potato, and biscuits served with a grey Riesling wine. Afterwards they all had Boston cream pie and ice cream for dessert. Later, they enjoyed Grand Marnier brandy and coffee.

They returned to Randall's room for a nightcap of Hennessy and then retired to their suites happy and ready for a good night's sleep before driving in their SUV the next morning to Newport, Rhode Island.

Dietrich picked Natalie up and carried her across the threshold into their suite. Natalie laid her head on Dietrich's shoulder and murmured, "Haven't we done this before?"

He kissed her lips and then said, "Yes, but not in Boston!"

He closed and locked the door and gently carried her into their bedroom and laid her on the bed where the covers had already been laid back with the customary gold-wrapped chocolate wafer.

"See, they already laid out the chocolates," he whispered. "You know what that means, don't you?"

She looked up at him and with a coy smile said, "No! What does that mean?"

"It means that Kira Ann wants us to work on bringing her back a baby brother. You do remember her request, don't you?"

Natalie reached up and put her arms around her husband's neck and nuzzled his ear as she pulled him down onto the bed and whispered, "Well let's get going!"

They melted into each other's arms and made passionate love until they fell blissfully asleep entwined in each other's arms.

18 THE NEWPORT TOWER

The sun was pouring through Natalie and Dietrich's glass balcony door revealing a clear blue morning sky. They were fast asleep still embracing each other when their telephone rang. Dietrich raised an eyelid and kissed Natalie on her cheek and then whispered, "Darling would you see who that might be so early in the morning?"

Then he looked at his watch and realized that it was almost nine o'clock. He jumped out of bed before Natalie could get up and again kissed her and said, "Don't get up, I'll see who it is."

He picked up the phone on the bedside table and answered, "Dietrich here, who is it?"

The reply was, "It's me, Randall. I just wanted to call and say that everyone else is still in bed and won't be up until ten o'clock, so you can get another forty winks of sleep and we'll get together at eleven o'clock in my suite where I'll have brunch served for everybody. What would you both want?"

Dietrich looked over to Natalie and said, "It's Randall and he said that everyone is still in bed and that we are getting together in his room at eleven o'clock for brunch and he wants to know what we want."

"Oh, you know. Eggs Benedict with strawberries and toast with orange juice and coffee and cream."

"Okay, I'm going to have waffles with New England maple syrup in addition to that. Okay?"

He turned back to the telephone to talk with Randall when he heard him say, "It's okay. I heard Natalie and you and I wrote your order down. Is there anything else?"

"No, I think that will do it. Natalie and I have to work on an order from Kira Ann."

Randall replied, "It's okay. I know it's a private joke between you and Natalie. Goodbye."

Dietrich crawled back into bed and curled up next to Natalie as she whispered into his ear, "It's no joke, darling."

At eleven o'clock, the adventurers had gathered in Randall's suite where breakfast had already arrived and was laid out by the hotel steward onto a table with five chairs.

They were still chatting about their trip to Newport when the steward announced to the group that their brunch had been served. Randall smiled and tipped the steward who smiled, nodded his head, and promptly left saying to everyone, "Bon appétit."

Lauren and her father had ordered poached eggs with toast, orange juice, and tea, and Randall had ordered a stack of pancakes with butter and New England maple syrup, bacon, orange juice, and coffee with cream.

It didn't take long for the conversation to turn to the topic of their goal that day to reach their Hotel Attwater at 22 Liberty Street, one block away from Touro Park and the Newport Tower and just a few blocks from the bay and marina. It is in the historic district close to the Newport Art Museum and Newport Tower Museum.

Allen was interested in getting up the next morning early enough to see the sunrise and watch the sun's rays as they passed through the square window on the east side of the tower. If the tower had some astronomical indicator, it was likely the sun, moon or Venus.

They finished their breakfasts and headed back to their

suites to pack their bags for the 71-mile trip that would take approximately one hour and twenty-one minutes if the weather and traffic conditions were good.

It took about thirty minutes for everyone to gather in the lobby of the Revere Hotel. Randall had already paid the bill and had valet service bring their Mercedes GLE 550e SUV around to the front of the hotel. In about five minutes, the valet had the vehicle at the hotel's entrance and the doors open for them.

Randall tipped the valet after all of the bags were secure in the rear cargo space and everyone had boarded the SUV for the afternoon trip to The Attwater Villa Hotel in Newport. From their hotel they were only one block from Touro Park and the Newport Tower. It was not a long trip, but the streets in Newport were very much like Old Boston where it looked like the streets had been laid out by cow paths, twisting and turning every which way!

After arriving in Newport the adventurers took their baggage inside The Attwater while Randall and Lauren parked their SUV. When they had all gathered in the lobby, they confirmed their reservations with the front desk clerk, received their key cards, and their bags were taken by a young porter, which they still called a bellhop, and were escorted to their rooms all located in the same area of the hotel. Randall tipped the bellhop for everyone who was surprised by the size of the gratuity and thanked Randall profusely.

Randall blushed slightly at all of this fuss and said, "Think nothing of it, son," and then shuffled into his room.

They had all agreed to assemble in a half hour in the lobby of their hotel and walk over to Touro Park and look at the Newport Tower. When they had previously driven by the park, they had noticed that there was an iron fence around the ancient edifice with a gate they would have to go through to see the structure. There was a custodian standing close by to help visitors or explain as best he could what they were observing.

After assembling, they walked with Randall leading the way. Allen and Lauren were close behind, and then Natalie and

Dietrich who noticed Meg's Aussie Milk Bar to the left as they reached Belleview Avenue bordering Touro Park. Dietrich announced to the group that Meg's Aussie Milk Bar sounded intriguing and that perhaps they should visit it on their return to their hotel.

It didn't take but a few minutes for them to get to the park and enter the enclosure around the ancient stone tower. Allen stood still as if he had suddenly seen Noah's Ark or the Ten Commandments. He took a deep breath and announced that he was overwhelmed. Randall was standing next to him with his mouth wide open in awe and staring at the tower.

Everyone was frozen and gaping at the tower when Lauren nudged Randall and said, "Didn't your mother ever tell you not to stare and to keep your mouth closed, lest a fly enter it."

Randall obediently quickly closed his mouth, and with a sheepish grin declared that she had indeed said that. Then everyone laughed. Lauren had broken the ice!

They slowly walked around the tower, and when they got to the west side of it, Allen noticed in the middle of the west-northwest exterior archway there was a tan colored granite keystone in the shape of the keystone, which is the symbol for the state of Pennsylvania. It is the same shape as the Frère Maçon mark for the master mason's keystone which would carry his personal mark on the keystone. It was only used for a very important construction and it was in west-northwest archway.

Lauren was beside her father when he made the remark and said, "Dad, look at that red granite orb-shaped stone above it. What does it remind you of?"

Before Allen could answer, Lauren said, "Remember what Betty Richards told us about her ancestor who married the daughter of the chief of the Mi'qmaq Indians? She said that the chief's daughter told her ancestor that the path to the treasure would only be revealed by the Venus window at the time of the harvest moon. Doesn't that red granite stone above the keystone in the arch look like a harvest moon?"

Allen replied, "Yes, I remember. Betty told us that that the story passed down in her family through the centuries also expressed that the chief's daughter was also in fear of her life if the secret was revealed to anyone."

By this time, Natalie, Dietrich, and Randall had gathered around Lauren and Allen.

Randall walked closer to the arch and looked closely at the keystone in the late afternoon light and said, "You know, I think you've got something there. I wish I had a ladder and a little more sunlight and a magnifying glass, but I could swear that there is a faint mason's mark on the upper half of that keystone that resembles the mark on the stone on the men's entrance to Rosslyn Chapel.

"I think you've found one of the important clues Lauren was talking about, and it is staring us right in the face! What was it that Jesus said? Oh yes. Let them with ears hear and those with eyes see."

They walked counterclockwise around the tower to the southwest corner when Lauren suddenly stopped and pointed up roughly halfway to the round second story of the tower where a single pure white quartz cobble stone was prominent in contrast to the rest of the stones in the construction. The stone was directly above the southwest column and to the right of the west square window in the second story of the tower.

She gasped, "That is deliberate. That stone is pointing southwest to something important. What could it be? Another piece of the puzzle. This tower was obviously very important and meant to stand the centuries. It is a major key and a lot more than it outwardly seems to be. If what we have just now discovered is correct and if Prince Henry Saint Clair and his men built it, the whole key to New Jerusalem may be standing right in front of us!"

Natalie quietly said, "Yes, Lauren is correct. This tower is oriented along a north-south and east-west axis. I think we need a compass to get the correct headings for what we are witnessing. This tower is like several buildings in one. It's an astronomical tower, a religious chapel with the eight pillars with windows oriented to the sun, moon and stars, and looks like it has Venus windows for when Venus rises in the east in the spring and in the west for the fall. This a master map for New Jerusalem and is also probably a navigational landmark—maybe even a light tower for ships!"

Dietrich put his arm around his wife and squeezed her shoulders and said, "I think she's got something. All of you are correct. This is something we are going to have to ponder. I can only imagine, once we start to examine this structure closely tomorrow, what we might find."

Randall sighed and said, "Let's go check out Meg's Aussie Milk Bar and see what it's all about. As Scarlet O'Hara said, 'Tomorrow's another Day.'"

Everyone was enthusiastic with their newfound discoveries and anxious for tomorrow to roll around. Nobody noticed the angry swarthy man, Mahmoud, on the Touro Park bench watching them. He had green eyes just like his twin brother, Mustafa. Mahmoud had been on the T-shaped pier in Fairhope, Alabama, watching with binoculars when his brother and his compatriot were being arrested. The temporalis muscles in his temples twitched with anger as he gritted his teeth and swore under his breath that he would exact a terrible price on these infidels for what they did to his brother, especially Lauren who was the skipper of the boat that ran down his brother, and Natalie who shot him.

The adventurers took no time finding Meg's Aussie Milk Bar and were delighted to see the very hospitable and friendly sign in the restaurant that declared, "Welcome to Meg's Aussie Milk Bar—C'mon In, Say G'Day and Grab some Tucker!"

Not only did they serve daily breakfast, but also soup and salad, hot sandwiches, fresh sandwiches and wraps, milkshakes and smoothies, expresso and quality coffees, and their specialty of hot meat pies.

Everyone was hungry and decided to have their evening meal in this delightful restaurant from Down Under.

They all splurged and each ordered a Caesar salad. Randall and Dietrich chose a Chunky Steak Meat Pie, while Allen chose the Australian Lamb Meat Pie, and Lauren and Natalie chose the Chicken and Herb Meat Pie for the main course. Randall also had a Bundaberg Spider Float Milkshake, Dietrich had the Banana and Strawberry Tropical Daintree Smoothie, Natalie and Lauren had the Gym Junkie Blueberry, Strawberry Banana, milk and Protein Smoothie, and finally Allen had the Splendour in the Grass Green Tea, Tropical Fruit, Spinach, Kale, Banana and Coconut Smoothie.

They were well-satisfied with their meals, the splendid service with friendly Australian humor, and left feeling full for the night and waiting in anticipation of what kind of an Australian breakfast would be waiting for them in the morning. They left the restaurant feeling good about their early finds.

On their way back to their hotel they noticed many passersby, the International Tennis Hall of Fame, the Audrian Auto Museum, and the Newport Tower Museum. The Redwood Library and Athenaeum were nearby, and there seemed to be a prominent police presence.

They felt safe, but did not know they were being watched by Mahmoud and two more of his accomplices, Abdallah and Braheem. The men kept well out of sight and only met late at night in a nearby town. They intended to discreetly watch and follow the group to the treasure wherever it might be. The Muslim Brotherhood had given up on trying to find the Templar treasure on their own. They had failed to get any usable information in Halifax, Miami, or even Fairhope where they lost brothers and a sister in the Brotherhood trying to find the secret to the Templar treasure.

Natalie, Dietrich, and Randall were asleep, but Allen was visiting with his daughter in her room discussing their finds at the tower for the day when he received a telephone call from his archeology friend in Istanbul, Dr. Peter Hawkins, a fellow archaeologist who was a partner in their last discoveries in Saint Sophia Mosque in Istanbul leading to Jerusalem and their quest for the Holy Grail mentioned in the Seton Family Secret manuscripts.

Dr. Hawkins said, "I thought I had better give you a call and let you know that I won't be able to meet with all of you in Newport, but wanted you to know that I did discover that in November of 2008, Steve Saint Clair performed laser measurements of the angles of lines projecting from the center of the tower, through the positions of the quartz cobbles and beyond. David Brody and Scott F. Wolter assisted him with this work and they discovered that the laser projection through the white quartz cobble above the southwest column pointed directly to the rüne stone found in the Mississippi delta.

"My hunch is that all of the rüne stone border markers for New Jerusalem found in the Mississippi Delta, Florida, Kensington, Minnesota, Oklahoma, Texas, the Missouri River junction with the Mississippi River, Iowa, and Oak Island are somehow connected with the Newport Tower, and somehow this is all connected with the Templar treasure taken by Prince Henry Saint Clair in 1398 to New Jerusalem.

"The tower in Newport was built to stand the centuries. It even survived a British attempt to blow it up during their retreat from Rhode Island during the Revolutionary War. All they succeeded in doing was blowing off the steeple roof when they blew up the second story floor and weakening the wooden porch around the second story. The heavily reinforced walls, except for the top one foot that the roof was anchored to, remained intact to this day.

"I'm sorry I won't be there if you discover where the treasure is ensconced, but my heart and soul will be with you. Tell your beautiful daughter I'm sorry I didn't meet her, and tell Dietrich to give Natalie a kiss for me. Natalie was such a dear in our quest for the Seton Secret."

Peter ended the conversation with "Take care."

Allen and Lauren said "Thank you and goodbye," and then he hung up.

Lauren was able to hear the conversation because Allen had put the speaker phone on for her.

"Well, that helped a lot," Lauren said. "I think we are pretty close to the solution. His remarks about the tower being the cryptic center for future explorations as well as expeditions for bringing new settlers to New Jerusalem is intriguing."

Lauren turned to her father and asked him, "Why weren't there later expeditions after Prince Henry's expedition in 1398?"

Allen replied, "We don't really know. There is some dispute about his voyages. We think that his exploratory voyage 0f 1396 was followed by another voyage with the twelve ships carrying the bulk of the Templar treasure that had been secreted to Scotland in 1307. He may actually have had more than the twelve ships.

"The Zeno narratives written later by his navigator, Antonio Zeno, mention several galleys of Sir Antonio Zeno on the explorations along with maps that he made for himself and Prince Henry. We do know that in 1396 Prince Henry made certain provisions for distribution of his wealth and properties. He transferred his holdings in Pentland to his brother, John, and he then drew up a deed that was signed at Roslin by his eldest daughter, Elizabeth, and her husband, Sir John Drummond of Cargill, where they renounced any claim they might have to his lands in Norway, which included Orkney and Shetland so long as Henry had male heirs. Thus, if he didn't return from his first voyage these lands would pass on to his eldest son, Henry II.

"Henry was not at the signing of the Treaty of Kalmar that united Denmark, Sweden, and Norway into one kingdom under the rule of Queen Margrette. He was represented by Bishop Jens of Orkney because he was away on his voyage of exploration. The ultimate goal he and Queen Margrette had was to extend the control of the three kingdoms across the Atlantic with the founding of New Jerusalem by Prince Henry Saint Clair. He had the full blessing and permission of Queen Margrette for this venture. It is also thought that his flagship for the voyage was Antonio Zeno's galley as suggested by the Westford Boat Stone. The Zeno brothers, Antonio and Nicolo, were noblemen from Venice and they also had a fleet of at least three galleys that accompanied Prince Henry's twelve ships.

"In October, 1412, Queen Margrette set sail on her ship,

Trinity, from Seeland to Flensburg for some meeting concerning her expanding kingdom. After returning to her ship from a meeting to strengthen her kingdom with the intention of leaving the port for home, she was struck down by a sudden violent illness which has been suggested by some as being poisoned by her enemies in the Hanseatic League. It has also been suggested that upon returning to Scotland in 1404 from his second voyage in 1398, Prince Henry Saint Clair was killed in a naval engagement somewhere off the west coast of Scotland by the same enemies of Queen Margrette to prevent the expansion of her Scandinavian Kingdom into the New World. Most certainly, Prince Henry had cannons aboard his ships since gunpowder was used for the first time in Europe during the Battle of Crécy in 1346."

Allen added, "You must remember that Prince Henry's daughter Elizabeth and her husband Sir John Drummond were the grandparents of Christopher Columbus' wife!"

Lauren had listened to her father in awe of his knowledge of history and said, "Dad, now all of this is beginning to make sense. Queen Margrette was trying to create a country that was later created by a band of rebels against England. A country that some of the founding fathers like Benjamin Franklin called the New Jerusalem."

"You've got it. What we refer to as the United States of America was actually conceived by Queen Margrette and was being carried out by her friend, Prince Henry Saint Clair of Roslin and Orkney. The only remaining records of the voyages to be found in Europe are the oral records of the Saint Clair family and a collection of letters and maps from Antonio Zeno in Venice.

"Prince Henry's grandson, Earl William Saint Clair, built Rosslyn Chapel as a memorial to Templar beliefs, the Saint Clair family tradition, and Queen Margrette's dream of a New Jerusalem in a shining land we now call America.

"Earl William left coded references to his grandfather's voyages in the carvings of American plants like maize corn and Aloe Vera within Rosslyn Chapel long before Prince Henry

Saint Clair's great grandson-in-law, Christopher Columbus, set sail for the New World with a copy of the Zeno maps!"

Allen looked at his daughter and remarked, "Remember that Major General Arthur Saint Clair from Scotland, who was on George Washington's staff, was working with Alexander Hamilton and Ephraim Brasher to make the first gold coinage for the new Republic."

Suddenly, Lauren jumped up from her bed where she had been lying while listening to her father's stories. She snapped her fingers and said, "Dad, you've just said the first key to the two-key box!"

Allen was surprised at her sudden revelation and said, "What are you talking about?"

"You know, Arthur Saint Clair—he's a Saint Clair and knew all the stories about his ancestors. He knew about the treasure and I'll bet he knew where it was hidden!"

Her words were tumbling all over each other as she gasped, "He KNEW where the treasure was hidden all along! Didn't you say that he was one of the major financiers that Washington had for the Revolutionary War? Where did he get the money to help? Did he bring it over from Scotland or did he get from the hidden treasure that his ancestor brought over in 1398? It's like the mystery of the Lost Dutchman mine in the Superstition Mountains outside Tucson, Arizona. Arthur Saint Clair is a big part of this puzzle and Alexander Hamilton and Ephraim Brasher were in on it too!"

Her eyes got big and then she asked, "Where did Arthur Saint Clair live when he came to America?"

Allen answered, "Greensburg, Pennsylvania."

He paused for a few seconds and then he stammered, "The Keystone State!"

They looked at each other and then they grabbed each other's shoulders and said in unison, "The tan keystone with the blood-red round granite stone symbolizing the harvest moon above it pointing west by northwest."

Lauren whispered, "Yes, but at what angle? We need a compass."

"Dad, do you have a compass?"

Allen said, "No, but I'll bet that Randall does. He always carries around that pocket compass that his maternal grandfather, Emerson Elliott, gave him when he was a youngster."

Lauren looked at her father and said, "Remember what Dr. Hawkins told you on the phone? You know. About the laser beam from the center of the tower through the position of the white granite stone above the southwest column pointing toward the rüne stone in the Mississippi River Delta which is one of the boundary markers for New Jerusalem. Do you have an ellipsoid map of the United States?"

Allen answered, "No, but we can find a map with latitudinal lines on the internet. Where is your iPad?"

Lauren ran over to her briefcase, opened it, and retrieved her iPad.

Her father said, "Don't we need a local network password to get online?"

She answered, "No, I have a new iPad that is connected to my wireless carrier and all I have to do is use that phone connection."

She quickly found a latitudinal and longitudinal map of the United States and said, "Let's take a look and see what latitude and longitude the Newport Tower is."

Allen had guessed what she was doing and already had his iPhone out and was looking it up.

He replied, "It's latitude 41.48.58 north and 71.30.99 west.

Lauren replied, "Okay, let's get a map of the United States and draw a line going from Newport, Rhode Island, in a west by northwest direction and see where it goes."

Allen got a piece of white letter paper out of the desk drawer in Lauren's room and held it up to the light. He could see through it. Then he asked Lauren to find a picture of a compass face on the internet so he could trace it in pencil on the paper as he held it on the iPad screen. Then he put the center of the compass over Newport, Rhode Island, on the map of the United States and with the edge of another sheet of paper traced a line in a west by northwest direction from Newport, Rhode Island, across the map of the United States to see where it went.

Suddenly, he gasped, "It goes to the middle of the western border of Minnesota in the general direction of Kensington, Minnesota, where they found the rüne stone marker."

He turned to Lauren and asked, "Could you look up the coordinates of Kensington?"

Lauren was already ahead of him and said, "It's at a latitude of 44.06.46 north."

"Could you look up the coordinates for Oak Island, Nova Scotia?"

Lauren queried, "Oak Island, why there?"

"There was a rune stone marker and a mysterious pit that had strange symbols. Remember how everyone thought it might be pirate treasure, but now they think that the engineering on the island was very skilled and may have been of Templar construction?"

Oh, yes, I remember now. Okay, I'll have the information for you in a second."

She quickly looked up the information and said, "The latitude is 44.30.46.9 north and 64.17.17.9 west.

They both looked at each other dumbfounded and then at the information she had just written. The parallel 44 degrees north was common to both locations.

Lauren stared at the numbers and said, "It's the northern border of Queen Margrette's New Jerusalem! New Jerusalem was the eastern half of the United States from the Mississippi River and part of Eastern Canada! But what does that have to do with George Washington's Doubloon and Ephraim Brasher's letter to George Washington?"

Allen thought for a minute trying to remember what Randall had told Christopher. "Oh, yes. He told him that the letter said that the doubloon was a valuable gift to the United States that Brasher referred to as the New Jerusalem."

Lauren replied, "That's interesting. That's what Benjamin Franklin called the United States.

I've never seen a picture of Washington's Doubloon or any of the other doubloons. Have you?"

Allen replied, "No, I haven't. Let's see if we can find any pictures on the internet. There ought to be some since Washington's Doubloon has been sold for several millions of dollars. Must be something unique about it from the others."

Lauren quickly searched the web and found pictures of both sides of the known Brasher Doubloons, including Washington's Doubloon.

As they looked at the doubloons, they noticed that Washington's Doubloon had E.B. stamped on the shield covering the American eagle's chest where all the others had Ephraim's E.B. initials on the right wing of the eagle's spread wings. That seemed to be the only difference.

Allen asked Lauren what the picture was on the obverse side.

She answered, "Dad, it looks like a mountain with a lake in front of it and a sun rising over the peak of the mountain. The mountain almost looks like a pyramid. There is some sort of an indentation half way up the right side of the mountain."

Allen said, "You know, that almost sounds like Masonic or Templar symbology. You know all of the people I mentioned were Scottish Rite Masons. What does the description of the sides of the coin say in the article with the pictures?"

Lauren replied, "It says the Washington Doubloon was a presentation piece especially struck just for George Washington and is the only one that has Ephraim Brasher's initials on the shield and over the heart of the eagle."

"What mountain is on the obverse side?"

Lauren replied, "The article says it is Mount Marcy at Lake Placid, New York, and the writing around the edges is the motto of the state of New York and the writing around the edges of the eagle side is the motto of the United States—E Pluribus Unum.

"Mount Marcy is the tallest mountain in New York State at the headwaters of the Hudson River and Lake Champlain between New York and Vermont. The article continues to say that the mountain was considered holy by the Great Spirit and by the Mohawk Indians who protected it from being desecrated."

Allen inquired, "What are the coordinates of Mount Marcy?"

"Let me see," Lauren said as she looked up the coordinates. You're not going to believe this. The latitude is 44.06.46 north and longitude is 73.55. 25 west."

Allen stared at his daughter and said, "Do you know what that coin is?"

And then he paused as his daughter smiled and said, "We've just solved the Gordian knot puzzle—IT'S A TREASURE MAP!"

Allen gave his daughter a big hug and then he asked, "Do you have a magnifying glass?"

Lauren replied, "We don't need one, I can enlarge the picture on the high definition screen of my iPad."

As she enlarged the picture the indentation half way up the mountain turned into a hooked X.

Allen stammered, "Quick, look up what is at that location on the mountain. Is there a map of the mountain?"

It took Lauren about a minute to find a map and see what was at that spot on the mountain signified by the hooked X.

"Dad, the map shows Indian Falls is at that location."

"Are there any pictures of the falls?"

"Yes. Oh, how disappointing. The falls don't look very big—maybe thirty-five feet at the highest. Maybe the opening for a cave is close by?"

Allen thought for a few minutes while he stared at the picture of Indian Falls.

"You know, I used to do some spelunking as a youth. Some of the caves had small openings before a small tunnel we had to crawl through opened up into a large cavern with stalagmites and stalactites. We need to go there and climb the mountain and take a look at it."

Lauren ran over to him and gave him a big hug and kissed him on his cheek.

Allen pretended to be embarrassed and dug his toe into the carpet and imitating Matt at the Back Forty Ranch said, "Shucks Ma'am, t'warn't nothing."

Lauren burst out laughing and said, "Do you think we ought to tell everyone tomorrow morning at breakfast that we have solved the riddle, or should we wait till we go to the tower and take all day to let everyone figure it out?"

Allen smiled and said, "No, let's tell them our theory and see what they say, and then if they agree, we can just eat breakfast at the Attwater Cafe and then check out and get on our way to Lake Placid. Maybe we can get some hiking garb there."

Lauren replied, "I'll bet so, dad."

They walked to the door to her room and he smiled as he turned around and said, "Love you," and then he walked down the hall to his room.

That night Lauren and her father got a good night's sleep with the satisfaction that they had broken the Gordian knot and solved the puzzle.

The next morning, the adventurers gathered in The Attwater Hotel Cafe for breakfast. The breakfast menu consisted of homemade baked goods and pastries, breakfast salads, granola, baked egg dishes, fresh fruit dishes, and juices and organic teas.

Natalie and Dietrich decided on orange juice and the baked eggs with lemon-ginger scones. Lauren decided to share with her father, Allen, orders of orange and grapefruit juice with baked eggs, cheddar-scallion scones, and corn muffins with raspberry jam, coffee for Lauren and tea for Allen. Randall had no willpower and chose a fresh fruit plate for everyone to share while he had the Brioche Au Chocolate with coffee and cream.

During breakfast, Allen invited Lauren to tell their friends about their discoveries of the night before. Lauren carefully detailed all of the events that had occurred and why she and her father had come to the conclusion the Washington Doubloon was actually a treasure map with Masonic and Templar symbology that pointed to Indian Falls on Mount

Marcy being the hiding place for the lost treasure. Even though the restaurant was near empty at this early hour, they spoke in hushed tones and Lauren used a note pad to elucidate key points in her presentation.

After she made her pitch to leave Newport and move on to Lake Placid immediately, the response from everyone was unanimous and affirmative to her suggestions. Allen beamed with pride watching and listening to his daughter explaining their conclusions and her leadership skills in planning the next steps for them to take. They agreed to go back upstairs and pack while Randall paid their bills at the hotel. Within an hour they had reassembled outside the hotel as their SUV was brought around for them to pack and leave.

Braheem was sitting in the lobby of The Attwater Hotel reading a newspaper when our adventurers assembled in the lobby waiting for their car to arrive. He immediately took his cell phone out of his pocket and called Mahmoud.

Mahmoud answered the telephone and said, "What's going on?"

Braheem replied, "They are all packed and ready to leave the hotel! I arrived here just as they were finishing their breakfast and going back to their rooms, and now they are all packed to leave and outside waiting for their car. What should I do?"

There was what seemed like an agonizingly long pause to Braheem, and then Mahmoud said calmly, "Go over to the clerk at the front desk and matter-of-factly ask the clerk if she knows where they are going. She might not know, but be calm and seem only mildly interested. Now go and call me right back."

Braheem obeyed and did what Mahmoud asked him to do.

The young lady at the reception desk said she didn't know, but the concierge overheard their conversation and told Braheem that one of the men, the Chinese gentleman, asked how far it was to Lake Placid, New York, and how long would it take and that he told him it was about 332 miles and would take five or six hours at this time of day. He said okay and thanked me and I gave him a complimentary map.

Braheem thanked the clerk and the concierge and then went back to the lobby, sat down, and called Mahmoud.

"What did you find out?"

Braheem answered, "The concierge said they were going to Lake Placid, New York, on Interstate 90 to Albany and then catch Interstate 87 to Lake Placid."

Mahmoud asked, "Are they still driving the silver Mercedes GLe hybrid SUV?"

"Yes," was Braheem's quick reply.

"Good! Get back here as quick as possible, and Abdallah and I will have our gear ready when you get back to the hotel."

19 THE PURSUIT

Braheem left The Attwater Hotel and sped back to their hotel where Mahmoud and Abdullah were standing in front with everybody's gear including Braheem's.

Braheem slid their 2018 black Audi Q3 Crossover auto into place next to the curb and opened the tailgate.

Mahmoud silently pushed their gear into the back of their auto and snarled, "Abdallah, you get in the back. Braheem, you drive and I'll do the navigation from the front passenger seat and let's see if we can catch up with them on Interstate 90."

Abdallah and Braheem silently obeyed Mahmoud and they were soon on Interstate 90 trying to catch up with their adversaries.

"Not too fast," Mahmoud cautioned, "We don't want to attract any attention or any police. Stay at the speed limit and pray to Allah that they will be going slower than us. We have some time to catch up with them. I just hope they haven't stopped for gas anywhere."

It was about an hour later that Braheem announced, "I think that silver Mercedes up ahead of us may be them."

Mahmoud said to Braheem, "See if you can get alongside them so I can see who is driving and then fall back a reasonable distance."

"Okay."

Braheem brought the Audi alongside the Mercedes for a second and then dropped back.

Mahmoud could see that it was Lauren driving, and as they dropped back he said to Abdallah and Braheem, "Good we've caught up with them. Now drop back several car lengths so they don't recognize us. I don't want to make the same mistake our brothers did in Westford. Their Mercedes has a superior camera system and I don't want them to know who we are."

When the Audi Q3 had pulled alongside, Lauren had noticed the same green eyes she had seen in Fairhope and told her father. Allen activated the Mercedes four corner cameras and was able to get a screen shot of the two men in the front seat of the Audi. He then called Steve in Edinburgh.

Katy answered the phone and said, "Hi, Allen. Steve and I were just leaving the office. What's up?"

Allen answered, "We are being followed by a black Audi Q3 Crossover and I got a snapshot of the front seat passengers. Lauren says she is sure that one of them in the front passenger seat is Mustafa, the guy Natalie shot in Fairhope."

There was a pause of silence and some muffled speech and then Katy said, "Allen, it can't be Mustafa. He's still in custody by the Homeland Security people in the United States. He is still in the hospital under close guard. Steve says it must be his identical twin brother Mahmoud who we thought was still in Jeddah, Saudi Arabia."

Natalie, upon hearing that said, "Oh, now we must contend with his brother!"

Katy and Steve heard that and then suddenly their images appeared on the dash screen so they could see each other.

Steve waved his hand and said, "Yes, that's correct. Allen, send me the picture you snapped. I should at least be able to identify the two guys in the front seats."

Allen said, "Okay," and then he sent the pictures to Steve.

Steve relayed them to Interpol for identification.

The I.D. came back in about two minutes and Steve replied,

"Yes, the person in the passenger front seat is Mustafa's twin brother and the guy driving is known as Braheem. The last time we saw Braheem was in London stirring up trouble. We thought he and Mahmoud were hiding out in Jeddah.

"There is a shadow of a third person in the back seat but we can't quite make him out for sure, even with photo enhancement, but our best guess is a guy named Abdullah, a close friend of Mustafa. If it is Abdallah, he is a time bomb that could erupt at any second. He is an assassin with a hair trigger personality. He likes to kill close up with a dagger like the ancient assassins.

"If you don't mind, I'm going to alert the CIA and Ari Shapiro who is working with them on loan from the Mossad. He is an expert on these very dangerous assassin actors, and besides, he has worked with you before. We pool our resources within NATO and the U.S."

Dietrich piped in and said, "No, Steve, we don't mind. We appreciate all the help we can get. As you have probably heard, we think we have an angle on the Templar treasure that left Scotland with Prince Henry Sinclair."

Steve answered, "Don't forget, we here in the U.K. have an interest in the treasure that left Scotland."

And then he laughed and said, "Treasure in this case will bring old friends closer together. We have your back in this venture and the queen has put high priority on us helping you. The Mossad, CIA, and MI5 are on board with you."

With that, Steve signed off and the occupants of the Mercedes SUV smiled as they looked at each other feeling safer than just a few minutes before.

Meanwhile, in the back of the Audi, Abdallah was complaining to Mahmoud and Braheem, "Why don't we just kill the infidels. There probably isn't any treasure and our mission should be to kill the infidels where we find them, just like Amin al Hussaini, the Grand Mufti of Jerusalem told Hitler. These Christians and Jews hang together and they should all be eliminated to bring about what has been ordained over thirteen hundred years ago—a Muslim World!

There was silence in the front seat as Mahmoud and Braheem listened to the ranting of Abdullah.

Braheem turned to Mahmoud and said, "He makes a lot of sense, why don't we just kill them or at least capture them and sell them in the slave markets. We have good contacts in the United States and we can drug them and pass them along to our operatives in Atlanta where they can be flown by charter aircraft to Rome and then on to the Middle East."

Mahmoud reminded his comrades that they and his twin brother, Mustafa, and his friend Ismail were assigned to find the treasure, and if it turns out there is none, then they can do whatever they want with Natalie, Dietrich, and their friends.

That seemed to satisfy Abdallah.

The black Audi Q3 Crossover kept a safe distance behind the adventurers as they were getting close to Lake Placid. Inside the Mercedes GLE Hybrid SUV, the dash high definition television screen suddenly came on. It was Ari Shapiro calling to say they had worked out a plan for their safety and stop the Audie Q3. They were going to be working with the New York State Police who would stop all automobiles for identity checks and searches two miles from where State Road 73 going to Lake Placid intersects I-87.

They will let your automobile through the check point quickly and detain the black Audie Q3 if they are still behind you. They are going to put up a flashing sign warning all motorists that two miles ahead and two miles from the intersection of I-87 and State Road 73 there will be an identity check and search of all vehicles and that everyone should be prepared to stop. This should either cause the Audie Q3 to turn around, or if they try to bluff their way through the checkpoint, they will detain and arrest them.

Ari smiled and then said, "We are watching them from satellites, and the State Police will turn their warning signs on when you are about a mile from the checkpoint. Good luck, I'll keep in touch with you later. David and I, along with a CIA officer, will be in Lake Placid with you, but you won't spot us."

The screen went blank and they all stared at each other.

Dietrich was the first to speak. He said, "International cooperation on these terrorists is a lot better than I thought."

Randall echoed his thoughts.

The time passed as the two cars sped toward Lake Placid. Just past Blue Ridge and the road toward Port Henry on Lake Champlain, the flashing warning sign of an inspection check two miles ahead came into view and Mahmoud said, "This doesn't look good. We're going to have to turn around and go to Port Henry and hide our car. It looks like it might be a routine check since we are so close to the Canadian border, but we can't take any chances. We may have to wait there and see if our comrades already in Lake Placid can find out where Natalie and her friends are staying."

Braheem looked over to Mahmoud and said, "It's good that you notified our brothers in Albany as soon as we found out from the concierge at The Attwater where they were going so they could go on to Lake Placid to get us a place to stay."

Mahmoud shook his head in agreement.

Their fellow travelers were American and had no trouble making it into Lake Placid. Now all they had to do was wait for Mahmoud to contact them so they could sneak them into Lake Placid from another route.

20 LAKE PLACID

Randall had called ahead and made reservations for their party at the Mirror Lake Inn at 77 Mirror Lake Drive in Lake Placid. It was a lovely five-star rated inn that has a panoramic view of the Adirondack Mountains and Mount Marcy, which is just a few miles from North Elba and the Adirondack Loj road to Heart Lake and the parking area to hike seven miles up the Van Hoevenburg Trail to Indian Falls on Mount Marcy.

The four-story historic old inn is located directly on Mirror Lake and has on-site dining and a spa. The Lake Placid Olympic Museum is less than 0.7 miles away and the inn has spacious suites and rooms.

Randall arranged for suites with balconies overlooking the lake for everyone. Fortunately, they were all conveniently located close to each other.

After checking in, the adventurers went to The View restaurant in the hotel where they had a fabulous dinner of seafood, filet mignon, fabulous salads, and desserts finished off with Hennessy brandy and Dutch Stroopwafels and coffee.

They were exhausted after the long day and were all anxious to go to bed and get rested for the next day. They had to get up and have a buffet breakfast before they went downtown to buy hiking gear for their climb up the mountain to Indian Falls.

Randall called Christopher in Texas and informed him of their discoveries. He immediately called Samantha, his secretary, and informed her that he had to leave right away on an emergency in Lake Placid and asked if she could arrange the necessary flights for him.

Sam, as he called her, immediately called Delta Airlines to get him booked on a flight that night from Austin's Bergstrom International Airport to Atlanta Hartsfield Jackson International Airport to Albany International Airport and then a private flight from Albany to the Lake Placid (LKP) Airport.

She called her boss back and told him, "If you hurry, I booked you on a flight leaving Austin Bergstrom in two hours with connections so you can reach Lake Placid tomorrow morning at 11 a.m., just in time for lunch with your friends at The Mirror Lake Inn. When I called The Mirror Lake Inn, they said Dr. Fox had already gotten you accommodations for the next three days at the inn."

Christopher replied, "I suppose he already arranged lunch."

Sam replied, "I wouldn't be surprised. But you need to get cracking and tell Carolyn that I feel for her and your last-minute getaways!"

Christopher turned to Carolyn who was standing nearby and said, "I suppose you heard all of what is happening."

She had a forgiving look on her face and said, "Yes, I'll go ahead and pack a bag for you as well as your hiking gear for the trip."

She had already been through all of this before since Christopher had been on mountain climbing expeditions with the New York Explorers Club many times before.

"You better take a shower and get dressed while I pack your bag," she said as she left the room and headed for their bedroom.

Balthazar, their cat, looked lazily up at both of them and then followed them to their bedroom and the bed he considered to be his.

In twenty minutes, Christopher was dressed and at the front door where he kissed Carolyn and rubbed Balthazar's ears. Carolyn was holding Balthazar in her arms as Christopher got into his Mercedes SL 550 roadster for the trip to Bergstrom.

On his way to the airport, Christopher called Randall and told him he was on his way and would call him when he arrived at the Lake Placid Airport.

Randall, who was already in bed, acknowledged his friend's arrangements and asked if he should buy him some hiking gear. Christopher replied that Carolyn had already packed his gear, and then he thanked him for getting him a room at the hotel.

Randall replied that he actually had not gotten him a separate room, but had arranged another bed be brought into his suite for him.

Christopher laughed and then said, "See you tomorrow!"

They hung up and Randall turned over and promptly went to sleep.

Randall and Allen both suspected there was some sort of cave, tunnel, or cavern somewhere around the falls, so they also were going to purchase Slyde King COB LED flashlights.

The next morning, they gathered back at The View restaurant at the Mirror Lake Inn and enjoyed their large buffet breakfast before going out and exploring the village.

They first stopped by the Lake Placid Olympic Museum to look at the displays. The last Winter Olympics there had been in 1980 where the United States ice hockey team on February 22 had beaten the much-favored four-time defending gold medalist Soviet Union ice hockey team. It was called "The Miracle on Ice." It was an interesting museum where they could have spent more time, but Dietrich reminded everyone that they needed to find a sporting goods store and buy their hiking gear for the next day's climb to Indian Falls.

They reluctantly left and soon found a store with all of the supplies needed. Randall made sure everyone had a very bright LED flashlight for cave hunting and exploring. They soon had all of the needed gear, sun glasses, shoes, clothes with long sleeve shirts and long pants, hats, rope, insect repellant, hunting knives, a machete, water canteens, MREs, and gloves.

The Van Hoevenburg Trail to the top of Mount Marcy is about fourteen miles long located in Keene, New York. Mount Marcy is 5,343 feet high and the highest mountain in New York. It normally would take about fourteen hours to hike to the summit. They estimated it would take them, with breathing stops, seven or eight hours to reach Indian Falls and search the thirty-five-foot-high falls and surrounding area for any cave or other area that might hide the treasure.

Allen said, "You know, we probably ought to be at the parking lot at Heart Lake by six o'clock in the morning to reach Indian Falls at a decent hour so we can be back at Heart Lake before nightfall. The trail is rocky with a lot of vegetation and some rock climbing which will be demanding."

Little did they know how trying tomorrow would be!

They returned to their rooms at eleven o'clock and put their gear in the closets for tomorrow's hike and gathered at Randall's suite to go together to the Cottage Restaurant in the Inn for lunch. Randall had already made the reservations for an extra place for Christopher who said he should be there for lunch.

Everyone was a little concerned because they had not heard from him, when Randall's iPhone rang and it was Christopher. He told Randall that his plane had just landed and he was about to deplane. Randall told Christopher he was on his way and would be at the airport in just a few minutes since it was only seven-tenths of a mile from Lake Placid. Randall excused himself and told everyone he would be back in about a half hour with Christopher and they would join them for lunch.

Christopher was patiently waiting for Randall at the airport reception area when Randall pulled up in the Mercedes SUV. They waved at each other as the SUV slid next to the curb. Randall pushed the button that opened the rear door and Christopher walked to the back of the car.

"You made good time," said Randall as he walked back to the rear of the vehicle while Christopher was loading his gear.

Christopher nodded his head as he closed the rear door and

said, "Yes, everything went smoothly. Sam sure knows her stuff. She made fabulous connections."

They shook hands and Randall remarked, "They just don't make people like Sam anymore. You sure are one lucky stiff!"

And then they both laughed because they knew that Sam was one-in-a-million and she would tell them so!

Christopher climbed into the front passenger seat of the SUV and they departed the airport for the hop, skip, and jump distance to the Mirror Lake Inn.

They arrived in a few minutes, and after parking and placing Christopher's luggage into Randall's suite, they both went to the Cottage Restaurant where everyone else was seated and had already received a before-meal drink to relax them before they ordered.

Natalie announced with a straight face to Christopher and Randall that Dietrich had already ordered a single-malt Scotch whiskey for them, but they were only able to get Glenlivet Scotch and she hoped they would be okay with that.

Everyone knew that was their favorite Scotch and smiled.

Randall feigned dissatisfaction and said, "Oh, that's too bad. I wish it could have been Lismore!" And then he laughed. Lismore would have been his second choice.

Christopher walked around and shook everyone's hand and said, I'm glad you waited on me. I wouldn't have missed this climbing expedition for anything. I even brought my own climbing pick!"

Lauren thought to herself, "Surely, the hike won't be that difficult?"

She didn't know how handy that pick would be the next day!

Christopher sat down and pulled his chair closer to the table and asked, "Now who was it who solved the riddle?"

Everyone looked at Lauren and Allen who were sitting together. Allen smiled and pointed his finger at his daughter and said, "She's to blame!"

Lauren's face turned red as she embarrassingly said, "Well, all I did was just mention that the doubloon was a treasure map!"

Allen then told the story of how they all went to see the boat stone and the Westford Knight which pointed to the Newport Tower where they made some discoveries like the keystone and harvest moon stone in the west by northwest archway.

He then related how Dr. Peter Hawkins had called from Istanbul and told them about how the white quartz stone over the southwest pillar of the tower pointed to the Mississippi Delta rüne stone, and then it became clear that the tower was the compass for the border stones of New Jerusalem.

He then described how it was only when they realized that the Indian legend of the harvest moon showing the way to the treasure and that the Newport Tower moonstone pointed to the Kensington rüne stone that we realized it was on the same latitude as the Oak Island marker. It was then that Lauren noted Mount Marcy was on that same latitude.

He then added, "When Lauren saw that the image of the hooked X was only on the image of Mount Marcy on Washington's Doubloon and no other Brasher Doubloon, she realized that Washington's Doubloon was really a treasure map.

"Since we saw the location of the hooked X was halfway up the mountain on the right side of the image, we looked on a trail map of the mountain and saw it was right where Indian Falls is located!"

Christopher was, indeed, impressed and said to Lauren, "Young lady, you are one smart cookie!"

Lauren blushed again, not knowing exactly how to take the expression.

Christopher noticed the perplexed expression on her face and said, "In my day that meant you are brilliant."

Lauren beamed, "Oh, thank you!"

Then she looked at her father who was smiling.

About that time the waiter showed up at their table and inquired, "What will everyone have for lunch?"

21 INDIAN FALLS

The morning broke the next day with a bright sun starting to rise on the horizon. The adventurers had already risen, had a hearty early morning breakfast, and just arrived at Heart Lake and the parking lot intended for hikers and viewers of the surrounding mountains of the Adirondack Mountains.

They had driven from the Inn on State Road 73 to Roger's Lookout at Heart's Lake at an altitude of 2,296 feet and parked their SUV. There was no one else there at that time, but that wouldn't last long since this was a popular trail. They had to hike up the mountain to Indian Falls which was at 3,608 feet over a rocky trail through timber-lined rock and gravel. They had to climb the 1,312 feet to Indian Falls carefully in the morning mist that hopefully would soon burn off. They felt lucky that it wasn't raining, which would have made their task more difficult. They only hoped that a sudden late May shower would not blow in.

Their route on the Van Hoevenburg Trail took them past Whalestail Mountain and Marcy Dam, about 1.1 miles from Heart's Lake where they could rest for a few minutes. Then they trudged on another 1.3 miles to the rear of Theodore

Roosevelt (TR) Mountain to Indian Falls on Marcy Brook and the Indian Falls Lookout at 3,608 feet.

Indian Falls is actually three falls tied together. The top ledge of the falls is fairly wide and tumbles its winter runoff water about thirty-five feet down to a ledge that extends out about fifty feet. Then the water flows over it onto a rocky ledge fifty feet below, then onward to a series of boulders extending at a forty-five degree angle to the side with a few fallen pine trees tossed against the boulders by the winter storms. The waters of Marcy Brook then curl around the base of TR Mountain to eventually blend with other mountain streams into a river that flows into Lake Champlain on the border between New York and Vermont.

The usual time for most average hikers taking a breather at Marcy Dam and TR Mountain is about seven hours.

Fortunately, it took the adventurers, working together with a rope line strung between them and a couple of fifteen minute rests, along with Christopher leading them with his pickax, less time than they had anticipated. Their mutual rope pulling helped each other over the rougher part of the trail. They were able to get to Indian Falls in less than five hours.

When they arrived at the three-tiered Indian Falls, they sat down and looked for a way to get to the top. After some discussion and Christopher's expert advice from his many experiences at mountain climbing and consideration of what effort it would have taken to haul heavy chests of gold and silver up the mountain, they mutually decided on a deer trail alongside Marcy Brook as the best way to look for a cave or tunnel that might be at the top of Indian Falls.

When they reached the top of the falls they noticed a natural ledge back and under the falls wide enough for two or three people standing side-by-side to walk behind the falls. They carefully inched their way up the deer trail alongside the falls to the level of the ledge. They could see it more clearly now and could easily step onto the ledge behind the falling water.

The ledge was now wet from the mist of the falling water, but during the winter when the temperatures dropped below freezing and froze the waterfall, the ledge could be cleared of snow and frozen ice so that two people could walk across it and carry a heavy load. The noontime sun made it easy for them to walk carefully behind the waterfall onto the ledge and examine the limestone wall of stone behind it.

They noticed there appeared to be the outline of an oval door about seven feet tall and six feet wide with large rounded red granite boulders on either side of the door's outline. The boulders were pressed against the edge of the door and the wall behind the waterfall and ledge.

As Lauren and Allen examined the outline of the door, Lauren looked up at her father and said, "Dad, do you suppose if we rolled those stones to the side of the outline and both pushed against the side of the door, it would rotate and open?"

Allen thought for a few seconds and replied, "You mean like what the ancient Chinese used to do, having a central balanced axis so the entire door would rotate leaving a three-foot opening on either side?"

Randall overheard them talking and said, "You know, that just might be the answer."

Then, after explaining Lauren's theory to them, Allen said to Dietrich and Christopher, "Let's see if we can roll those round stones to the side and rotate the door and open it."

The three of them struggled but were able to roll the stones to either side of the door's outline, and then after a pause, they caught their breath and collectively pushed inward against the right side of the outline of a door in the wall and nothing happened. The next time, all six of the adventurers pushed and there was a creaking sound as the door moved an inch inward.

They all looked at each other with amazement, and then they pushed again—it moved another couple of inches!

They moved back, caught their breath and then pushed again in one mighty effort and the door swung open to reveal a carefully carved tunnel in solid stone. It was about eight feet tall and six feet wide. There were torch holders on either side of the tunnel with ancient wooden torches still inserted in the holders waiting for someone to ignite them.

Natalie noticed a faint odor of pitch emanating from the torches and remarked, "If it's what I think it is, those torches are soaked in pine tar and would ignite in a New York second!"

Everyone took in what she had just said and then they all started to laugh.

Randall cleared his throat from laughing and said, "Well, hello! It took us a third time to open the door, but only once for Natalie to spring the ultimate joke and say it in a New York treasure tunnel!"

Allen quipped, "Hold on Randall, we haven't seen any treasure yet."

With that they all turned on their LED flashlights and walked down the tunnel. As they walked farther, they could hear the distinct sound of running water, and about 200 yards down the tunnel they could see the wide opening of the tunnel into a cavern with stalactites and stalagmites and a running small underground river bed with water flowing across the floor of the cavern and suddenly falling over a ledge in a cascading waterfall inside the cavern.

They also noticed more torches and torch holders around the sides of the cavern.

Randall asked if anyone had any matches and Christopher said, "Yes, I think I have a waterproof container in an emergency pouch on my climbing belt. He searched the pouch and found some waterproof matches and walked over to a tar soaked torch and lit it. Suddenly, the cavern lit up with light and they could vaguely see a large quantity of chests lined up on the cavern's floor.

Everyone let out a gasp!

Dietrich said in hushed tones, "The treasure of the Knights Templar that my ancestor Shönfeld mentioned in the manuscript we found in Saint Mary Chapel at the Thirteen Sycamores. I just knew the legends in my family history were true!"

Everyone took their flashlights and each ran to a torch holder and returned with a torch and held them next to the torch that Christopher had ignited.

One by one, they lit other torches in the cavern with their torches and then returned their torches to their holders.

The cavern blazed with light and everyone could see better now. There were hundreds of chests piled up evenly in stacks in the center of the cave. They walked over to the stack of chests and pulled several from the heap.

Christopher walked over to the stack of chests and pulled one of the smaller ones down onto the floor where it burst apart with ancient gold and silver coins scattering out onto the floor of the cavern. They were mostly Greek and Roman.

When they opened a few more chests with Christopher's climbing pick, they could see that the gold and silver coins were from many ancient civilizations including Egyptian, Phoenician, and Jewish coins from Jerusalem. They even found some from China!

Allen looked at one chest that Christopher opened and stammered, "These necklaces and bracelets are jewelry from Persia and India and maybe even ancient Troy. What are they doing with all of these medieval coins and jewelry?"

Randall said, "The Knights Templar dealt with many peoples and empires. Don't forget they were the bankers of the ancient world!"

He added, "We need to extinguish these torches, close the tunnel door, and return to Lake Placid where we can celebrate our find and later after we catch our breath, report our find as soon as possible to the United States authorities, and then inform the University of Texas authorities and the New York State authorities. This is an important find that reaches back many centuries and deals with many peoples, including the Mohawk and Abernaki Indians that had kept the secret over the centuries."

He no sooner had said this when a raspy voice echoed across the cavern and the adventurers turned to behold Mahmoud, Braheem, and Abdallah who stood in the tunnel at the entrance to the cavern.

Mahmoud and his minions, holding AK-74 assault rifles, walked over to the adventurers and smiled.

Mahmoud grinned and said, "Thanks for finding the Knights Templar treasure for us!"

He laughed loudly, so his laughter echoed around the cavern and crashed against the walls.

Abdallah and Braheem joined in, and soon Abdallah, in a loud voice yelled, "Enough of this nonsense, let's just cut their heads off and leave their bodies for the animals."

Braheem looked menacingly at his brother terrorist and in a loud voice said, "Are you crazy, let's just rape the women and sell them all on the slave block. Why not make some money off them? The two women would sell at a handsome price and the four men would make good laborers in Africa."

Mahmoud turned and looked at his haggling accomplices and said, "No, my brother Mustafa, who was arrested in Fairhope, wants these people to suffer like he has suffered. Our leaders in the Brotherhood want the treasure so we can use the Crusader's fortune to help us conquer the world for Allah! It would be sweet revenge for the Crusader's crimes against our people. Using their wealth to enslave their people would finally be sweet revenge!"

Natalie shuddered at hearing this diatribe. She suddenly realized the resemblance of Mahmoud to his twin brother with the green eyes who tried to kidnap or kill her in New Orleans and Fairhope. She then noticed his terrifying green eyes and then a shudder went down her spine.

She looked at her husband Dietrich, who had a defiant look in his eyes and was gritting his teeth and clenching his fists.

Suddenly, Abdallah screamed in an evil voice and shouted, "No! Vengeance is mine! Allah has found me and wants me to behead these infidels. It's my mission and I must obey!"

Abdallah pulled his machete from his belt and rushed aggressively toward the adventurers, and heading straight for Natalie as his first victim.

Natalie stood firm and refused to cry.

Mahmoud leveled his AK-74 and shot Abdallah in the head effectively decapitating him, and then he looked at Braheem as if to say, "I'm in charge and you will obey me."

During this time, Dietrich and Randall noticed that Christopher had taken advantage of the incident with Abdallah and pulled his climbing pick from his belt and was in the act of throwing it at Mahmoud. As Mahmoud turned back to his captives, Randall and Dietrich rushed Braheem. Dietrich attempted a tackle while Randall threw himself toward Braheem, who by this time had moved close to the waterfall pouring over the ledge in the cavern.

Braheem sidestepped Dietrich slightly, losing his balance when Randall grabbed him by the waist, pushing him toward the waterfall.

In the same instant, Christopher had thrown his climbing pick which caught Mahmoud cleanly between his green eyes causing him to wildly discharge his AK-74 in a chatter of random bullet fire, one of which hit Braheem in the back of his head, shattering his skull. The other bullets from Mahmoud's AK-74 bounced against the ceiling of the cavern smashing one of the stalactites, causing it to fall as Mahmoud fell backward onto the cavern's floor.

The momentum from the rush by Dietrich and Randall and one of the stray bullets from Mahmoud's assault rifle hitting Braheem in the back of his head caused Braheem and Randall, who was firmly holding Braheem around his waist, to fall into the rushing water of the underground river. Both were swept over the ledge of the waterfall and fell onto a limestone ledge forty feet below.

Randall didn't have time to scream as they both fell silently to the ledge. When everyone realized what had just happened, they ran over to the edge of the waterfall and saw the two bodies lying silently on the ledge with Randall lying face down on top of Braheem, still holding onto Braheem's motionless body.

They aimed their flashlights onto the two bodies and could detect no motion from either Braheem's or Randall's silent bodies—not even any breathing movement or sound was noticed.

Christopher, Dietrich, and Allen looked down upon their

friend's body thinking about how, in an attempt to save them, Randall had given his life to these evil terrorists who were a scourge to humankind.

Natalie and Lauren were holding each other, and silently, tears ran down their cheeks.

After a few minutes of realization about what had occurred, they knew that the only thing left to do was extinguish the torches and close the door to the entrance of the tunnel, roll the locking red boulders back into place, and call Steve.

After they rolled the boulders back to lock the closed door, Dietrich called his friend to inform him what had just happened. It was eight o'clock in the evening in Edinburgh when Dietrich called and Katy answered the phone. When she heard about Randall's death, there was sudden silence and then a gasp as Dietrich heard Katy telling Steve what had just happened.

Steve got on the phone and said, "I'm terribly sorry to hear about Dr. Fox's death, but happy to hear that everyone else is safe and the lost treasure of the Templars has finally been found. I am going to call the deputy director general at MI-5, Sir Richard Bothwell, so he can phone the queen and tell her that one of her knights in the Venerable Order of Saint John has died during the recovery of her majesty's lost Templar and Order of Saint John treasure that was taken from Scotland."

After Steve again expressed his regrets over what had just happened, he said, "Let Katy and me know when and where Randall's funeral is going to be so we can fly over to the United States for it. Okay?"

They both hung up and Dietrich relayed to every one of the remaining adventurers what Katy and Steve had said.

Allen was distraught and said to Christopher, "I think we should inform the president's office about what has just happened so they can deal with the issue of the Templar treasure find in New York since the queen of England will no doubt have something to say about the treasure."

Christopher looked at Allen and the rest of the adventurers and said, "Hell, No! I'm going to call the president himself!"

22 THE EPILOGUE

Katy and Steve Grant, along with Rania and Anton, had come over to Fairhope and Cliff House to meet with Lauren, her boyfriend, and Allen. Rania and Anton had named their twin children, Maria and Jan, after Natalie's parents and her mother, who was also named Maria. Peter Hawkins and John Zachary Bartholomew had also arrived for the meeting of old friends to talk about and exaggerate their adventures.

Carolyn and Christopher even had their cat, Balthazar, who was confused over the invasion of HIS house.

Peter Hawkins and John Zachary Bartholomew agreed and co-occupied the last guest room in the house since they had not brought their wives. It was like a convention of old warriors and their spouses and children getting together. They were all saddened that Randall was not there to tell his jokes or tease Kira Ann or tickle Rania's and Anton's one-year-old twins. He had loved children, even his own whom he rarely saw.

The saddest part of the whole affair at Indian Falls had been when the police arrived the next day at the cavern to gather the bodies of the slain terrorists and Randall, they found that

Randall's body was missing while the terrorist Braheem's body was still on the ledge forty feet below the cavern's river falls.

Randall had simply disappeared, and even though the search of the cavern's river and its outlet at the base of Mount Marcy revealed no trace or evidence of Randall's body, the only evidence of his death was Christopher's photograph of his friend lying on and partially next to Braheem right after he had fallen with Braheem over the edge of the falls.

After everyone went onboard Carolyn and Christopher's yacht, *The Columbine,* for a picnic and a cruise around Mobile Bay, they sailed down toward Cliff House and a seaward look at the *Ecor Rouge.*

Rania and Anton had left their twins with a friend of Carolyn's and Christopher's at Cliff House while they went on the sailing picnic.

Everyone thoroughly enjoyed themselves that day. That night after dinner at Cliff House, Allen remarked that probably the reason for some of the empty chests they found was that the gold was probably used by Alexander Hamilton and his successors to make Brasher Doubloons which were used to settle the national debt incurred during the Revolutionary War, Jefferson's purchase of the Louisiana Territories, and the War of 1812. It was the Templar gold and the secret of Washington's Doubloon that made it possible for the United State to be completely debt free in 1838 when the Treasury Department closed the Indian Falls gold mine and the treasure trove within and sealed it for future use.

America was debt free until the Civil War in 1860, but by that time, the story of Indian Falls and the story of Washington's Doubloon had been forgotten. Washington's Doubloon was passed down through Washington's heirs and later rediscovered in the late 1800s along with six other Brasher Doubloons that had not been melted down or lost. The doubloons that were shipped abroad to settle America's national debt to other countries were melted down by those countries to make their own coins.

Allen sighed and said, "Politicians then, as today, have only expedient memories!"

Everyone relaxed after Allen's explanation of the lost gold mine and treasure.

John Zachary Bartholomew looked at everyone and mentioned a story he heard about the Civil War and its aftermath and Reconstruction of the South. John Zachary's thoroughly entertaining history monologue about the end of the Civil War was followed by him talking about the mystery surrounding the lost treasury of the Confederate States and its cover-up by the Knights of the Golden Circle.

Lauren spoke up and asked, "Who were the Knights of the Golden Circle?"

John Zachary mused about the loss of the lost gold of the Confederacy Treasury after the Civil War and the fall of Richmond, its capitol.

He said, "There were tales about its disappearance after it was seen being offloaded from the train carrying it from Richmond to Washington, Georgia. It was offloaded from the train onto several wagons in plain view by more than thirty witnesses and just disappeared, never to be seen again!"

Natalie interjected and laughed as she said, "Does this mean, like my husband Dietrich used to say to Randall at the end of one of their capers, the game's afoot again, my dear Watson?"

23 ABOUT THE AUTHOR

FRANK R. FAUNCE

Frank R. Faunce, DDS, is a retired colonel in the United States Army. He was an associate professor and Pediatric Department chair at Emory University School of Dentistry in Atlanta, Georgia. He was the last Command Dental Surgeon of the Third United States Army and served overseas in that capacity in most of the Middle Eastern countries and in East Africa. He was commissioned as a captain during the Vietnam War and was activated for overseas duty during Operation Desert Storm. His last duty assignment overseas was in Mogadishu, Somalia.

Dr. Faunce graduated from Marion (Indiana) High School in 1956 and attended Purdue University for one year, studying mechanical engineering, before graduating from Indiana University in 1960. He graduated from the Indiana University School of Dentistry in 1964. After serving in the United States Army during the Vietnamese War, he completed his residency in pediatric dentistry in 1974 at the University of Texas Dental Branch in Houston. He served as deputy director of the Dental Division of the Academy of Health Care Sciences at Fort Sam Houston in San Antonio, Texas, and on special assignment to the United States Army Institute for Dental Research at Walter Reed Army Hospital in Washington, D.C. He also has been a consultant to the Office of Technology Assessment established by Congress. He commanded the 333rd Medical Detachment in Savannah, Georgia, and has been awarded the Meritorious Service Medal with Three Oak Leaf Clusters and the Presidential Order of Military Medical Merit.

He also has been made a Knight of the Military Order of Saint Gregory the Great by Pope Benedictus XVI and an Officer of the Most Venerable Order of the Hospital of Saint John of Jerusalem by Queen Elizabeth II. He is also a Knight of the Order of Saint John of Jerusalem, Knights Hospitaller, and was made a Knight Bachelor by King Peter II.

He has written many scientific papers and articles and a textbook on aesthetic dentistry. He has been interviewed on national television and radio, and articles have been written about him and his research in national and international newspapers, magazines, the Saturday Evening Post, and the Encyclopedia Britannica. He was a consultant to the American Dental Association on aesthetic dentistry, served as president of the Academy of Dentistry International, is a fellow of the International College of Dentists, the American College of Dentists, the European Academy of Prosthetics, and the American Academy of Pediatric Dentistry, and is a member of the Board of the Academy of Pediatric Dentistry.

He has several patents and has lectured extensively at universities in the United States, Canada, Mexico, Europe, and Asia. He is a Distinguished Alumnus of the Indiana University School of Dentistry and Marion High School, and is an Honorary Citizen of New Orleans.

Dr. Faunce's military experience and his travels throughout Europe, Asia, Middle East, Africa, and North America provided the background for this timely novel that is replete with vivid imagery that gives the reader a sense of being there.

22902639R00109

Made in the USA
Columbia, SC
05 August 2018